Family Dynamics

A Randall Arthur Novel by

DeWayne Twitchell

Copyright © 2024 by DeWayne Twitchell

Published by Flock Publishing, a division of Pink Flamingo Productions

All rights reserved.

No part of this book may be reproduced in any form or by any electronic or mechanical means, including information storage and retrieval systems, without written permission from the author, except for the use of brief quotations in a book review.

Edited by Paige Editorial Services

Formatting by Ebony's Formatting Collective

Cover designed by MiblArt

For my two families.

All happy families are alike; every unhappy family is unhappy in its own way.
—Leo Tolstoy
Anna Karenina

Sin? What is sin inside the dynamic of family relationships? It is a mystery that began with man. No one can solve it except through his own unique experience. How you feel is human. But do not think it will leave you alone. We are never free of our blood.
—Leon Uris
Redemption

I just wish I could understand my father.
—Michael Jackson

Chapter 1

TUESDAY
January 2020

The Void was approaching...

That was how he imagined the harsh reality of death now within the recesses of his stroke-damaged mind. Not a transition into an afterlife so desired for millennia by the human psyche—as long as it didn't involve fire, brimstone, or any eternal agony. But the Void, with a capital V. Because he was now of the belief, after long and often psychologically painful soul-searching, that there was no Heaven, no Hell, and no place where all the souls of the deceased—good or bad—would live. No place that both Mother Teresa and Adolf Hitler could call their eternal spirit home. No conscious afterlife of any kind. Just a great nothingness, much like the one before his conception.

Joseph Bowles was resigned to the impending end of everything he had accomplished, experienced, and felt. But what he wasn't resigned to, what he couldn't fathom, was how his eldest son, who now stood at his bedside in tears waiting for his father to die, could have betrayed him in the manner he had done, after all the parental love and support Joseph had given him.

He wanted to say something to him now, but the stroke had stolen his ability to speak.

He tried to transfer his hurt and hatred from his heart into his eyes, but he didn't know if it registered. He was so weak.

Let me die! Oh, please, let me fucking die! Let me die so I won't have to feel this goddamn heartache anymore!

Roger Bowles and his wife, Nancy, were the only ones with him now in the ICU of Lakeshore Hospital in Falcon City, New York. The doctor had seen Joseph an hour ago and told Roger and Nancy that there was nothing more modern medical science could accomplish and that the end was near.

A nurse had been in about ten minutes ago to check the weakening vitals of the near-dead patient and left Roger and Nancy alone with Joseph. Their two teenage children had been there earlier to bid their grandfather farewell. It was just too bad about Bryan, but he had made his choice long ago and had held to it. He was a member of this family in name only. Roger had not invited his brother to the hospital to say farewell to his estranged father and had not even informed him of what had happened.

In his time of dying, Joseph thought of the son he had lost. He was thinking of Bryan when the stroke struck him because Bryan was now Joseph's only hope to salvage what damage would be done by his brother.

Joseph had set events in motion before the stroke. However, the stroke prevented him from finishing what he had to do in totality. But he hoped that what he had been able to do would be enough to initiate action.

He could hear the cold beep of the heart monitor grow

fainter, slower. He knew what was coming and was brave enough to accept it and whatever came after. Even if it was eternal non-existence.

And if he reached a fiery Hell, could it be worse than the suffering that Roger, who had ostensibly always stood by him, had laid upon his heart—the same heart that had already experienced enough heartache in his lifetime? And could Heaven truly make that suffering meaningless? For the first time, Joseph was glad that his beloved wife, Tara, was dead, so she would not have to bear her heartbreak over her son's betrayal, even though she died because her husband had broken her heart.

Roger and Nancy's kids were still around, young, and hopefully just in the early stages of long and happy lives. But if they discovered what their father had done, how would they deal with the pain?

That thought further hurt Joseph's heart that those two innocent children should have to suffer for the sins of their father and grandfather.

The last thing Joseph Bowles saw was Roger and Nancy standing above him, both with tears in their eyes, arms around one another. Joseph's last physical sensation was the tears leaking from his eyes.

Goddamn you, Roger. Why couldn't you just let it be?

The Void arrived.

Approximately ten minutes after Joseph Bowles drew his last mortal breath, his son Roger, after the requisite tears and hug with Nancy, got into the elevator and descended to the first floor and the lobby of the hospital. He no longer wept or needed to weep, at least for the moment. Dressed in a heavy winter coat, he walked out hurriedly and stopped under the awning of the entrance, a frigid wind blowing in off Lake Ontario. It was shortly after 5:00 P.M., and it was already dark. He removed his iPhone from his coat pocket, went to his apps, found the one he needed (indicated on the screen only by a black-shaded triangle icon), and activated it. The man he was calling had described this relatively new app to him weeks ago, shortly after their meeting. He explained that it had been created by the brilliant men and women at DARPA and that the CIA was presently using it. But he had connections and could access it for him, with a called-in favor or two.

Without getting into the techno mumbo-jumbo, he said that once the app was activated and a number dialed, the subsequent conversation would be scrambled, unable to be understood by anyone who might be secretly listening. Then, once he was sure the app was working, Roger scrolled through his phone contacts until he found the number he wanted and speed-dialed it. Roger just had to wait a few seconds before connecting.

"It's me. The son of a bitch just died. It's time to begin your mission," Roger said, checking around him to ensure no one else was within hearing range. Thankfully, few people were willing to brave the cold.

He disconnected without waiting for a reply from the other end.

Sorry that you're going to miss all the fun, you old, dead bastard.

Family Dynamics

"You seriously like this show?"

Connie Shidler sat on the living room couch in her home in Flagstaff, Arizona, next to her sister, Stephanie Winslow, looking over at her husband, Jay, sitting in an adjacent chair to the girls' right. They watched a *Duck Dynasty* rerun on A&E on their 52-inch, wall-mounted, high-definition television. "Well, yeah. Everyone seems to love this show. Look at the ratings."

"I don't love it."

"Why?"

"Well, let's see, first of all, even though it is supposed to be a 'reality show,' you can tell it's scripted. Like all so-called 'reality shows' are. Second, these people are just a bunch of moronic hillbillies from the South, including the one who openly thinks all gay people are going to Hell unless they change their supposedly sinful ways. Those bastards deserved to lose the Civil War. Third, they supported that fascist, racist, dumbass motherfucker Trump, who, God knows how, ended up being elected president. And fourth, who cares about a bunch of hillbillies that make duck calls for a living?"

"You're just jealous because you're not as rich and famous as they are," said Stephanie.

"No, dear sister-in-law, I'm not jealous."

"Denial's not just a river in Egypt," said Connie.

"And that has to be the stupidest fucking saying of all time," replied Jay. "And I'm not jealous of those people, and I'm not in denial. It's a stupid show, contributing to the dumbing down of this country. And if I'm in the minority in that opinion, fine with me."

Before this argument on 21st-century pop culture could continue, Jay's smartphone on the small table to his right chimed, the ringtone being the shrill synthesizer opening of "Separate Ways" by Journey. Jay picked up the phone and looked at the number displayed on the screen with no facial reaction.

"Excuse me a moment, ladies," Jay said as he rose from the chair, answering the phone on his way down the hallway and into the bedroom. Even though he was now out of sight of the two sisters, they could hear the bedroom door close.

"You know, I love Jay and all, but he can be such a pain in the ass sometimes," said Stephanie.

Connie laughed. "I love him, too. And, yeah, he can be a pain in the ass. But he's been a great husband, even though he's away on business so much."

"Yeah, I know. And, I hate to admit, a great brother-in-law, too."

"You know what they say about men being from Mars and women being from Venus?"

"Well, Jay is definitely a Martian."

Connie laughed again. "Ain't that the truth? And I don't care what he says, *Duck Dynasty* rules. Especially Jase. He's freakin' hot!"

"Damn right, sister!" They high-fived at that proclamation.

Both heard the bedroom door open. Jay had come out with his right hand behind his lower back, and before either of the women could ask what the call was about, Jay brought his hand out from behind his back as he entered the living room. In that hand was a SIG Sauer Mosquito semi-automatic pistol, a silencer attached to the barrel. Both hands were covered with latex gloves.

Before either woman could even produce a scream, which

Family Dynamics

Connie was in the first moments of uttering, her eyes beginning to widen in shock, Jay aimed at his wife's head and shot her with the cold, steady hands of an expert Olympic shooter going for the gold.

Then, in the space of less than half a second, he executed a brief arm sweep toward Stephanie and shot her in the same manner before either could completely register what was happening. The two sisters ended up sitting on the couch, leaning away from each other, heads destroyed, blood and brain matter staining the upholstery.

Then, just because he felt like it, Jay turned toward the television with Jase Robertson, duck call expert and redneck sex symbol, presently on screen. He quickly aimed and shot twice at the image, causing sparks to fly.

Luckily for Jase, who was probably still at home in Louisiana, he didn't suffer the same fate as the sisters in Arizona. All he did was disappear from Jay Shidler's sight, his face being the last image ever displayed on that screen.

Once the need for gunfire had ended, Jay Shidler went back into the bedroom and reopened the closet door, where he had retrieved the hidden gun from its locked case on the top shelf. He placed the SIG on the dresser and kneeled to remove several cardboard boxes from the floor, moving them over to the carpeted bedroom floor. Underneath these boxes was tile flooring. Four tiles were a hidden latch to a compartment Jay had secretly built into the floor.

He took out a pocket knife from his jeans pocket and, using the blade, stuck it in the tile's groove to allow him to lift it. Once the door was up, he took out what he had hidden inside—a large duffel bag full of the materials he would need for the coming days.

He unzipped a section of it and took out a black mask, which he pulled over his head. He took out one more item—an envelope that would help give him the time he needed to do what he had to. By the time the authorities figured out the truth, it would not matter to him.

He zipped the bag back up, shut the door, replaced the boxes, closed the closet door, grabbed the duffel bag by its strap, and walked out of the bedroom for the last time.

Back in the living room, he placed the envelope between the bodies of the two women in plain sight. Looking at their bloodied corpses, he thought, *Dying in the living room—what irony*. Then he turned around and walked toward the door near the laundry room, which led into the garage.

He opened the garage door by the remote on the wall, got into his silver 2015 Hyundai Elantra, placed the duffel bag on the passenger seat, started up the car, and calmly drove it out of the garage, heading out of town in the fading light of late afternoon. He didn't even bother to close the garage door. If there were neighbors outside, he wanted them to see the car with a masked man escaping the premises, making it appear, perhaps, that something nefarious inside had occurred.

Which it had.

This had been in the works for some time, and he had repeatedly reviewed the operation in his head, hoping to work out every kink that might rear its ugly head. His travel plan had already been mapped out. Jay Shidler had a long journey ahead.

He would be heading northeast.

Chapter Two

Not long after the sad death of Joseph Bowles, that evening, Randall Arthur, his lovely twin sister, Rachel, and Randall's best friend, Larry Carter, had braved the terrible January weather—nearly ten inches of lake effect snow on the ground, an unforgiving cold wind, and a nighttime temperature of fifteen degrees above zero Fahrenheit—to attend the East Coast Hockey League (ECHL) match between the hometown Falcon City Blizzard and the Kalamazoo Wings. Fortunately for all the fans and the two teams, the city street workers had mostly cleared the roadways and parking lot of snow and ice, so getting to and from Lakeside Arena wouldn't be too much of a problem. And it was lucky for all concerned that they were in the lull between the previous snowstorm and another one, which was supposed to hit town late tomorrow night. However, the citizens of Falcon City were accustomed to this inconvenience. The city was on the southern shore of Lake Ontario, and its placement always put it in harm's way of those pesky lake effect storms. The community had learned to deal with it while dreaming of spring and summer and the baseball games on the vibrant green grass of historic Red Givens Field, just east of the arena on the lakeshore.

They were seated near the ice, three rows back. Before the game and after the organist had played the national anthem, the public address announcer had informed the crowd of the death of the long-time publisher of the *Falcon City Expression* and Blizzard supporter, Joseph Bowles, and had asked for a moment of silence amongst the gathered. Then the game got underway. The first period was near its end, and the game was scoreless. Both goalies were in fine form so far, rejecting good shots from entering their respective nets with quick minds and agile reflexes. So far, the game was free of penalties, with several hard but clean hits.

Randall was seated to Larry's left, with Rachel to Larry's right. "Do you guys want anything from the concession stand between periods? It's on me."

Larry thought about it for a moment. Then he looked over at Rachel. "A couple of hot dogs sound okay to you?"

"Sounds good. And a couple of Cokes, too, Randy."

"Okay. I'll get a hot dog and Coke for myself, too. I'll get them after the period's over."

This happened about a minute later, both teams leisurely skating off to their dressing rooms to the slight cheers of the crowd, still knotted at zero. Randall got up to return to the concession area, along with many others who had the same notion. As he walked up the steps, he heard Larry and Rachel giggling in their seats. He looked back toward them. They had their heads near each other in conversation, like lifelong friends. Which they were—sort of.

Family Dynamics

They'd known each other since childhood, as long as Randall and Larry had known each other. But Randall thought of Larry and Rachel's relationship more along the lines of acquaintances. They were friendly because Larry and Randall were best friends, nearly brothers. And since Rachel was Randall's sister and lived in the same town, she was on the periphery of the two men's friendship. But that sure as hell did not look to be the case since last summer. It had been a steady progression. The three went to Falcons baseball games last June. Then, starting in November, Randall and Rachel went to see several Falcon City High School basketball games because Larry was beginning his first season as head coach of the varsity. At these games, Randall could not help but notice that Rachel cheered for Larry's team more enthusiastically than even her brother had. It caused Randall to wonder if things between them were changing from simple acquaintances to something more substantial. Yet he had said nothing to either, fearing that he was being paranoid and that they would think the same and subject him to friendly but still embarrassing ridicule. And they had said nothing to him of a change in their relationship. Hell, maybe he was letting his overactive imagination rule. Or perhaps he wasn't ready to accept the possibility that Rachel and Larry were becoming more than platonically chummy.

Randall reached the concession area and found the queue at the counter. There were already ten or fifteen people ahead of him. He settled at the tail end of the line of fellow hungry and thirsty humanity and patiently waited to progress up to the front. A few minutes passed when a man dressed in a Falcon City Falcons baseball cap (the bill was down just low enough to shade his eyes partly), a black winter coat, a gray T-shirt, blue jeans, and sneakers came up to his right. "Excuse me, sir," the man said as he lightly laid his left hand on Randall's arm.

Randall turned to look at the man. "Yes?"

The man lifted his cap just enough to see more of his face above the nose. "Pardon me, but are you Randall Arthur?"

Randall grinned. "Guilty as charged."

The man laughed at Randall's funny rejoinder. "My name is Bryan Bowles." He extended his hand to Randall.

Randall took it. The name sounded familiar. "You're the cartoonist who draws that comic strip, *Family Dynamics*, right?"

Bryan smiled. "Guilty as charged."

"And who's related to the Bowles family that owns the newspaper?"

"Yes. Joseph Bowles was my father. And, yes, I'm sure you're wondering why I'm at a hockey game with my family tonight in a half-assed disguise of a ball cap instead of mourning."

"Yeah, to be honest, the thought did cross my mind. I'm sorry to hear of his passing."

"Thank you. Actually, that's why I wanted to speak to you. I know you're a professor at Falcon City College, but I saw your ad online about your private investigation business, and I need a private investigator." He gestured with his head toward the entryway to the stands, where a lovely red-haired woman stood holding a young girl with matching hair, perhaps a year or two old, and another slightly older adorable little blonde girl standing closely beside her mother and little sister. "My family and I are here for the game, and we saw you and your friends down a few rows from us. I had been thinking about calling you, but we saw you here, and my wife suggested I approach you and ask if you would help me out. This concerns my father, whom I was estranged from, partly explaining why I'm here."

"Well, sure, I'd like to help you if possible. I'll be home from college tomorrow afternoon at around four o'clock. That's where I have my PI office. You could come by then, and we'll talk more about it if you'd like. Do you recall the address from the ad?"

Bryan nodded. "Yeah—corner of Fourth and Underdown. Four o'clock is fine with me. I appreciate you seeing me." He shook hands again with Randall.

"No problem. I'll see you tomorrow. Enjoy the rest of the game."

"Thank you. Same to you." Bryan walked back toward his family, and Randall finally reached the concession counter, where, from a pretty, late-teen girl in a red and blue uniform comparable to those worn by workers at fast-food joints, he bought three hot dogs and three Cokes.

As Randall descended toward the seats with his bought fare upon a cardboard tray with the stylish Blizzard logo printed on the bottom, he thought about his potential new case. He wondered why Bryan Bowles, whom Randall was shocked to see at a hockey game the same day as his father's death, would need Randall's services. But Bryan said that he and Joseph had been estranged, which explained some of Randall's questions but certainly not all. He assumed he would find out more tomorrow.

As Randall approached his seat, carefully balancing the tray's contents to prevent the food and drinks from spilling all over the steps or someone on either side of him, he saw Larry and Rachel still talking and laughing. He had to admit to himself that, despite his initial shock, they looked like a cute couple—a couple that belonged together.

But my best friend and my sister?

If this were true, this would be a major life change.

Chapter Three

Jay Shidler arrived at the Super 8 Motel on 450 Paisano Street in Albuquerque, off Exit 166 and Interstate 40, at precisely 8:33 P.M. on Tuesday, five hours after murdering his wife and sister-in-law. He had called ahead to ask for any vacancies, and the desk manager told him they had several. Jay and Roger Bowles had designed this trip, estimating travel times on maps online, looking at motels online that could be reached by day's end. They knew the plan was most likely fluid, considering things that might happen along the way. But for the moment, after a call to Roger one hour after leaving Flagstaff, the plan was to stay in Albuquerque tonight, drive most of the day tomorrow to Topeka, Kansas, drive all day Thursday to Columbus, Ohio, and then drive to Falcon City from there, arriving sometime Friday afternoon or evening. He had ditched his Hyundai Elantra at a crowded mall parking lot in Gallup, New Mexico, and found the new rental car placed there by one of Roger's minions a few hours prior. It was a silver 2017 Nissan Altima with New Mexico plates. Jay found the keys under a magnet just under the left bumper. He took his duffel bag, unlocked the trunk with the fob, and placed it inside. He then unlocked the front driver's door with the same fob, got in, started it up, and left the parking lot, continuing eastward.

Once he had reached the motel, he parked his new car in the parking area and walked into the front lobby with his one duffel bag across the lighted lot, under the porte-cochere. The only person in sight at this late hour was the desk manager. Jay knew it was not the one he had spoken with earlier. That had been a young gentleman named Scott, and this person was a pretty brunette in her mid-to-late twenties. Her name tag read *Teresa*.

He walked up to the desk and stood on a rug with a giant Super 8 logo embossed upon it. He told Teresa that he had called earlier and asked for a room overnight and that Scott should have left a note to confirm. Teresa didn't have to look for the note because before Scott had left for the evening, he'd told her to expect a gentleman named Robert Welsh around 8:30 to check in for the evening. That was the name Jay was checking in under.

There would be different names at different motels. Jay had even produced several debit cards with different names to show the desk clerks at the motels for validation in case he needed to. All the cards had money on them, but he would only use them when paying cash was impossible.

He showed Teresa the card with the Robert Welsh name and a fake New Mexico state ID and signed the Welsh autograph in the register. At the same time, Teresa did some quick typing on her computer and he paid cash upfront for an overnight room until about eight tomorrow morning, when he'd be leaving. He even prepared a story about the quick in-and-out overnight routine.

He was traveling to El Paso, Texas, for a funeral. A close college friend had succumbed too early to the cancer monster, and he had a fear of flying and enough time to get to El Paso in time for the funeral while traveling on America's highways, where he didn't have to worry about possibly falling miles to a fiery death in case of catastrophe.

Teresa made her saddest face and told him she was sorry. She found the digital key card to his room and gave him directions to get there. "If there is anything you need, sir, don't hesitate to call."

Jay thanked her for the condolences, the directions to the room, and the offer of assistance and walked across the carpeted lobby to the elevator.

Jay went up to the second floor, meeting no one on the way. He figured they were in their rooms for the evening or out and about on the town for the evening. He quickly found the room and scanned the lock with his card to open the door. The room was nice, with a single bed, HD television (not as large as the one in his home that he had shot, along with his wife and sister-in-law), and a window view of the outdoor pool covered with a tarp for the winter.

He undressed, placed his clothes in his bag, and took a long shower. Even though he felt no guilt about killing his wife and sister-in-law, he felt a need to symbolically wash the action out of his system by cleansing his skin as thoroughly as he could. Whenever the bodies were found (which Jay figured had already happened or would soon happen because he thought Stephanie's husband would have been frantically trying to contact her and set things in motion from there), they would find the letter that he'd carefully written in Arabic, explaining that Boko Haram, the terrorist group out of Nigeria, had exacted revenge upon Mr. Jay Shidler, former mercenary of Blackwater, for killing several of their comrades-in-arms in the rather conflicted region of northern Nigeria, and that punishment was due.

The two women lying on the couch were in the wrong place at the wrong time. The video that Jay and Roger had requisitioned weeks ago revealed three masked men garbed entirely in black, two of them with swords brandished on either side of the other man, on his knees, hands tied behind his back, in helpless supplication, and in the background a white wall with the large, black Boko Haram standard with white Arabic lettering hanging from it. This video would hit social media tomorrow. And while those who saw it would believe Jay Shidler to be in the hands of an Islamic terrorist organization, about to meet his violent death, Jay himself would, in reality, be traveling on the American interstate highway system by day and by night, staying in motels, until he reached Falcon City, New York, to execute his mission. After that, he would be out of the country for good, presumed dead at the hands of Boko Haram once the second video of his beheading was released.

After his shower, Jay put on a pair of white briefs and retired for the evening. He set the alarm on his smartphone to sound off at seven in the morning. He planned to be checked out of the motel and on the road again by eight.

CHAPTER 4

Chapter 4

WEDNESDAY

Randall had been home just twenty minutes from his teaching day at Falcon City College. He was washing a few dishes left in the sink from this morning in the kitchen, which he didn't want to bother placing in the dishwasher, while looking out the window at the yard blanketed with deep snow, with more to come later. An ash-colored sky and a present temperature of twenty-five degrees held no promise of better things on the way. Randall wished that spring would hurry and arrive.

Bryan Bowles was five minutes early for his appointment with Randall the afternoon after their initial meeting at the hockey game (won by the Blizzard, 3 to 1). Randall saw a blue Chevrolet Aveo gingerly pull in next to Randall's Ford Taurus in the snow and ice-laden driveway, which Randall had sprinkled liberally with rock salt after the first storm. Randall dried his hands with a dish towel and opened the door as Bryan reached the front porch, pounding the snow off his boots on the concrete.

"Hello, Bryan. Come on in."

They shook hands. Bryan was wearing a pair of black leather gloves. "Thank you. The less time out in that cold, the better." They reached the kitchen, and Randall said, "Come on upstairs to my office."

"Sure thing."

As he took off his gloves and stuffed them in his overcoat pocket, Bryan followed Randall through the kitchen and dining room, then left down a short hallway, then another left up a short flight of stairs to Randall's PI office.

Randall turned on the ceiling lights and showed Bryan to one of the chairs. "Please take off your coat and have a seat, Bryan."

"Thank you." Bryan removed his overcoat and Blizzard cotton scarf, revealing a thick blue and white cotton sweater. He draped the overcoat and scarf over the back of the neighboring chair and sat down.

Randall sat behind his desk. "So, how are you today?"

"Fine, thanks. Cold as hell, though."

Randall chuckled. "Yeah. This isn't exactly the Caribbean, is it?"

"Nope. They're saying another ten or eleven inches of snow tonight."

"Yeah, I heard earlier on my car radio. More damn shoveling tomorrow morning."

"Tell me about it. Listen, I'm glad you could see me before the storm hit."

"No problem. So, what's going on?"

"Well, as you know, my father, Joseph, died yesterday afternoon at Lakeshore Hospital as a result of a massive stroke. And, as I told you last night, I've been out of his good graces for the last few years. My wife and kids are unfortunately included in that. My brother and the rest of the family —Roger's wife and kids—have shut us out, as well."

"Oh—I'm sorry to hear that."

"Don't be. If you had the family I ended up with, you'd want to be estranged, too."

"May I ask what happened?"

Bryan sighed. "Well, to make a very long and complicated story short, I didn't want to have anything to do with the newspaper business. My brother is still part of it. However, I wanted to be an artist. Loved the idea ever since I was a kid, especially comics. The newspaper business just didn't interest me. I knew I'd be miserably unhappy if I even gave it a shot. My father didn't take that very well and said that if I insisted on pursuing what he called 'my childish pipe dream' and didn't take my rightful place in the family business, I was no longer to be a part of the Bowles family. He told me to give up my dream or leave the family. So, I left. I pursued my career as an artist, got lucky and syndicated my comic strip, and have done pretty well for myself and my family—my wife and two daughters. The one true family I feel that I have."

"Seems rather cold on your father's part. And obviously, your brother was on your father's side in all this."

"Oh, yeah. Roger has always sided with his daddy, no matter what. Anyway, my father disowned me. He wrote me out of his will completely. You might have noticed that *Family Dynamics* doesn't appear in the *Expression*. My father always said to other people that having his son's comic in his paper would be nepotism. That wasn't the real reason, though. He didn't want to add to my success, certainly not having my strip in his paper. I heard about my father's death on the evening TV news. Not a phone call from my brother. Not an email or text message. Nothing. We have yet to be invited to the funeral." He smiled a little. "I'm not expecting us to be.

"But yesterday morning, hours before Joseph died, I got a call from an attorney here in town, Burt Olivetti. The odd thing is that he's not even the family attorney. Anyway, he asked me to come to his office because he had something that he wanted me to see." Bryan reached over to the adjacent chair for his overcoat and pulled out an encased DVD from an inner pocket. "This is what he wanted to show me. When my father had his stroke two days ago, he was in Mr. Olivetti's office, recording this. The disc shows my father collapsing. By the way, this was how I learned of my father's stroke. We briefly considered skipping the game last night after hearing about his death but went anyway. If not for the estrangement, it would have been different. But we didn't consider my father a true member of our family anymore...which was his choice. Mr. Olivetti told me that my father wanted me to have this and that he did not want Roger to know about it." Bryan looked over to see Randall's small nineteen-inch HD TV and combo DVD/VCR player on a rolling stand. "I'd like for you to see it."

"Certainly." Bryan gave the case to Randall. Randall got up, walked over to the stand, popped the DVD out of the case, turned on the player and the TV, and slipped it in. Randall returned to his chair, and he and Bryan waited for the recording to begin playing. Bryan had seen this three times previously and wasn't enjoying a fourth go-around. As Randall would soon see, it was disturbing.

The image showed Joseph Bowles sitting in a comfortable, high-backed leather chair in Burt Olivetti's office. Joseph did not look well. His color was bad. He looked much older than his age. To Randall, he looked like a man who had suffered a broken heart.

"Hello, Bryan," Joseph began, his voice somewhat shaky. "I hope with all my heart that you are watching this. I know I have no right to ask you what I am about to ask, but I don't know where else to turn." He pauses, looking down at his lap. He takes a deep breath. "Mr. Burt Olivetti is recording this for me. I did not want to go to Mr. Holbrook for this for reasons that I will soon make clear. I have asked him to give this to you in case something happens to me." Another pause. "And I have a distinct feeling that's going to happen soon. I haven't been feeling well lately, Bryan. Your brother does not know about this recording, and he cannot know. That is why I have employed Mr. Olivetti's services. Mr. Holbrook is also Roger's attorney, and I don't trust him anymore. Like I said before, I don't know where else to turn.

"Before I go on with anything else, Bryan, I want you to know I'm sorry for any pain I have caused you. I know that won't make up for what I've done to you, but it's all I have to offer. I still cannot understand why you didn't want to be part of what has built this family. You are a very bright man, Bryan. You could have been a great asset to the *Expression*. I still think you made the wrong choice despite your success. And I will go to my grave believing that. The worst part of our estrangement has been that I haven't seen my grandchildren. I'm sure that they are both beautiful little girls. They are both innocent victims of our problems, Bryan. And I certainly don't hold that against them.

"Bryan, I need your help." Joseph stops. On the recording, it can be clearly seen that he has started to cry. He pulls himself together, but his voice is still shaky. His eyes are blinking rapidly, perhaps in response to the tears. "Your brother is about to do something that will destroy the family. It has already destroyed me." He has now lost control of his emotions, crying as Bryan has never seen his father cry before. "Bryan, you have to stop him before it's too late! Stop him." Then he gasps. His eyes roll back in his head, and he falls forward out of his chair. Another voice is heard offscreen. It is Burt Olivetti's voice saying, "Oh, Jesus." He comes into view to kneel beside Joseph. He checks him for a pulse. He then removed his cell phone from his suit jacket pocket and dialed 9-1-1 for help.

"You can stop the disc now," Bryan said to Randall. "There's nothing else we need to see. Just Burt performing CPR on my father."

Randall grabbed a remote control from his desk and stopped the DVD player. "Wow. That must have been a trip to watch."

"To say the least. It's hard to watch someone have a stroke, despite how I might feel about him."

"When was the last time you spoke to your father?"

"Probably about thirteen years ago or so. Around that time, I was still in college and told him definitively that I would be an artist."

"So, this man who has disowned you dies, but before he does so, he leaves you a DVD recording to let you know your brother has done something terrible, and he wants you to fix it."

"But he collapses before he can tell me what he was supposed to have done. That's why I came to you."

"You want me to try to discover what he did."

"If you're able."

Randall smiled. "Depends on how hard it will be to find out."

"Well, considering how well I know my family, it won't be easy. But I figured that a professional private eye would have better luck at it than an amateur like me."

"Is there anything else you can tell me about your family that might give me some idea of what I might look for? Have you heard any gossip or anything about the paper or your family?"

Bryan shook his head. "No. I've been out of the loop regarding business and family matters for several years now. And I didn't care about that until the disc came into my life yesterday."

"Roger's been the publisher for a while now, hasn't he?"

"Yeah. Roger took over the *Expression* operation about three years ago when my father finally decided to retire from that part of the business. My father still retained ownership, but Roger runs things for all intents and purposes. Since my father's death, I assume Roger is now both publisher and owner of the paper."

"I know that your mother committed suicide. At least, that was the story released by the family."

Bryan nodded. "Yeah—back in 2003. She was manic-depressive. Not sure what pushed her over the edge. She left a note, but it just said she couldn't deal with the pain anymore and that she loved us and hoped we could forgive her. I was still in college but was told not to come to the funeral, that I wasn't welcome. My mother and I stayed in touch. She was the only one who would. She was the only one who understood my decision. The damn newspaper didn't control her life as it did my father and still does my brother."

"Did you forgive her for what she did?"

Bryan sighed. "It took me a bit to understand why she did it, but I guess now maybe I get it. Mental illness is an ugly thing to have to deal with. And so was my family."

"Have you thought about what could have driven your father to contact his estranged son? What could Roger have done? Something connected to the paper? Or maybe personal?"

"I've wracked my brain. He would've told me on the disc if he hadn't had that stroke. At first, I considered doing nothing. My thought was that I owed my father nothing after the way he treated me. Not just me, but my wife and children. He didn't contact my two little girls to be the grandfather he claimed he wished he could've been. He thought my wife was a big part of why I insisted on pursuing cartooning instead of helping run the newspaper, which is true. She encouraged me to be my own person, to do what I loved to do instead of what my family wanted me to do. So that made her as *persona non grata* as me. Now, suddenly, the selfish old man wants my help. Screw him."

"So, what made you change your mind?"

"My wife, again." Bryan smiled. "They're always called the better half for a reason. She had the wisdom to point out to me that maybe my dad was trying to tell me that he trusted me above anyone else when the chips were down. He discovered that Roger wasn't to be trusted for whatever reason. Sadly, whatever was bad enough for him to take the desperate measures he took. So maybe, despite all the crap that happened in the past, I should at least help him to make things right finally. Or at least as close to right as I can."

"Okay, I'll take the case. I'll do what I can to find out what your father was trying to tell you before his stroke. I can't promise positive results, but I can promise I'll do what I can."

"Thank you. If I may make a suggestion, you could start by speaking with Mr. Olivetti. He was the only other one in the room when the recording was made. After that, just use your best professional judgment, I guess."

"I'll call him tomorrow. I'm assuming that the snowstorm will cancel classes at FCC, so I'll have some time off from my classes to do some investigative work." He had a thought. "You know, once I start snooping around, your brother will eventually find out about your father recording that DVD."

"That's fine. And, by the way, you can keep it. It's the only copy. I've seen it enough. It will be sort of fun to see Roger sweat a little."

"Roger doesn't have a lot of good feelings for you, does he?"

"No. And the feeling is mutual. His entire life has been consumed by making his daddy happy and making the newspaper successful. My point is my wife and kids mean everything to me, and I would never sacrifice that for success and glory. Like my father, Roger just cannot understand why I would turn my back on my blood family for another that I started on my own. However, considering that my blood family is dysfunctional as hell, you can understand the decision I made. They want nothing to do with me, and until now, I've wanted nothing to do with them. All this over a goddamn newspaper and me wanting to draw funny pictures for a living. I'm going to do this one last thing for my father. After that, I'm done with them forever."

Chapter Five

Bryan Bowles had left Randall's office about an hour after arriving, having settled on a payment schedule for Randall's services. Randall would call Burt Olivetti tomorrow, either at his office or home, depending on whether the blizzard would hamper his travel to work. After that, he would play it as he went.

It was well into the early evening, and the snow had yet to start falling. Randall was in his downstairs office, doing his non-private investigative work. For this PhD in history, it was grading papers, preparing tests or lectures, or writing books that were artistically accomplished but that only some people read because he self-published them on Amazon. He could only promote them to a certain extent without the big budget of a New York City-based publisher backing him.

Presently, Randall was working on a final draft of a book he had begun last year about the history of shipping on the Great Lakes, from the primitive indigenous people of the area to the days of wind-propelled sails and finally to the present period. He had enjoyed working on the project, but he was already keen to start something that had engaged his mind since being brought to the front burner by a conversation with Larry one night while watching *Sunday Night Football*.

By the middle of the third quarter, the game was a boring blowout, and while Al Michaels and Cris Collingsworth were forced into seemingly endless banter to keep what was left of the viewing audience attentive and from switching over to something else more entertaining, Randall and Larry had discussed other matters. Larry brought up the subject of the American Revolution because he had just started teaching it to his high school class, and he mentioned the name Haym Salomon. He was a Polish merchant and banker who had immigrated to the colonies and ended up helping to finance the effort of the rebels to break free from the chains of Britannia. Larry pointed out that Salomon was mentioned less often than people like Washington, Jefferson, Adams, or Revere. Randall agreed with this assessment, and the seeds were planted for Randall's next book.

He had gone to both the college and city libraries to find any books that might have the name of Haym Salomon within them. There weren't that many. He was a little more successful on the Internet, which had more information on Salomon, and he had made copies of that information for his research. He also realized that if he wanted to produce the best book he could on this subject, he would have to travel to Salomon's birthplace of Poland. Sadly, he couldn't do that until late spring or early summer, when his teaching duties were done for the semester. He had already made plans to do just that, maybe spending as long as a month in Poland to learn more about this obscure man who had captured his intellectual imagination.

In the meantime, Randall had to complete the present project, and after seven months of writing, he was nearly at the finish line. He was writing the final chapter. After finishing that and a final personal edit, he'd turn it over to Patricia Sherman, the editor he hired for his books before he self-published them to the Amazon Kindle store, for her input. After months of mental tussling with several choices, he had finally come up with a definitive title for the book.

This new book was to be called *Plying the Five Lakes: A History of Shipping on the Great Lakes*. It wasn't going to rock the world like if it had the name Harry Potter in its title, or if it involved teenage vampires, or if it were about a rich but troubled man who liked very kinky sex, but it would be good enough for him.

Randall's cell phone, resting next to his computer, rang. He saw the number and name on the caller ID screen and hit the answer icon. "Hello."

"Hey, Randy. It's me." The "me" in question was Andrea Rutherford, once a student of Randall's at FCC, now a part-time research assistant on his current project.

"Hey, Andrea. What's going on?"

"Not much. How about you?"

"I'm here in the downstairs office doing some finishing work on the book and waiting for the snow to arrive."

"Do you think the college will be open tomorrow?"

"I seriously doubt it, sweetheart. Last I heard, the snow was definitely on its way, and it will probably be worse than the last storm we had. Buffalo is already getting hit with it. So,

I would safely bet the house that there won't be. Why do you ask?"

"I have some research material for your next book on Haym Salomon that I copied off the Internet and from material I found at the FCC library. I was going to either bring it over to you or give it to you when you were at FCC."

"Don't worry about it for the time being. With the bad weather coming, it's not a big rush. If you want to wait a few days, that will be alright."

"Okay, just let me know when you want it, and I'll pass it on."

"Sounds good. Talk to you later, dear. Stay warm and safe."

"You, too. Bye."

"Bye." Randall hit the disconnect icon and placed the phone back on the desk. Andrea approached him at the end of the spring semester last year when the World War II class that he had been teaching, which she was a student, had concluded. She confessed her lust for him and her fervent desire to act on that lust. He had said yes, and subsequently, they had sex around fifteen different times. The sex was phenomenal, and they both loved every second, but he had been having misgivings about this no-strings-attached sexual relationship. The main problem was that he cared for her but didn't love her, and she didn't love him. And that was okay with them both. But he knew in his heart that this could not go on long term and that the fire was ebbing. Last spring, he wanted no strings attached, but after a few months, Randall and Andrea felt maybe it was time to end that part of their relationship, enjoying the memories of that time but moving on to platonic friendship. It had been a long time since he had lost the love of his life, Pamela McFarland, because of that damned freak drug overdose back when they were both in high school, and he had consciously held himself back from a new serious relationship. He had thrown himself into his work, whether academic or law enforcement and investigation and it mainly did the job. But he still had that empty place in his soul that needed to be filled. And, as much as he was attracted to Andrea, he knew she wasn't the one. And she had also known it and agreed to end things, with them remaining good friends and with her helping him out on research whenever he needed.

Randall continued typing at his workstation for several minutes after he had hung up from Andrea's call when the cell phone signaled again.

Randall saw the number on the ID—Larry. Randall answered. "Hello."

"Hey, Randy."

"Hey, Larry."

"Busy?"

"Yes."

"Oh. Sorry."

"It's okay. Just working on the book. What's up?"

"I was just going to let you know I wouldn't be over tonight. Just in case you wanted to do something else. I don't want to get out in the snow and get stuck at your place. No offense."

"None taken. Smarter to stay at home tonight."

"Hey, I had a great time at the game last night. Hope we can do it again soon."

"Yeah—me, too. I'm sure we'll hit the next home game. A week from tonight, isn't it?"

"Yeah." Larry was silent for a moment. "Rachel seemed to have a good time, too. Don't you think?"

Warning bells started going off in Randall's mind. *Where is all of this going?* "Seemed to me she did. Both of you."

"Yeah. She's a terrific lady. Despite being related to you."

"Haha, smart ass. Despite that heavy burden she must bear for the rest of her life, she is a terrific lady, indeed." Randall considered whether to bring the subject up and eventually jumped into the dangerous waters. "The two of you seem to be getting rather close lately."

"Well, Randy, I've always liked her."

"Yeah, I know that, but it seems the two of you are spending much more time together in the past few months."

"Mmmm. Well, I guess maybe that's true. She's just a great person to hang out with. You know, like you are."

Randall then heard someone clearing their throat in the background.

Wait a second. That sounds faintly like a female. And it sounded vaguely familiar. *No, it couldn't be.*

"Larry, is someone there with you?"

Larry didn't reply immediately. "Ah, no. Why do you ask?"

"I thought I heard someone clearing their throat. A woman."

Larry laughed, but it sounded nervous. "I think you heard the TV. I have that on now."

"Oh." Randall could hear a television playing in the background. But, no, that cough was not from the television. It was *Rachel*! He had heard her do that many times before in his life and had the sound of it etched in his memory. Rachel was at Larry's house!

Before Randall could say anything, Larry said, "Listen, I have to go. Nature's calling and it's *really* insistent. I'll talk to you tomorrow, okay?"

"Yeah, okay."

"Enjoy the digging of snow in the morning."

"You, too. Bye, Larry."

"Bye." Randall had wanted to tell Larry to say hello to Rachel for him, see what his reaction would be, but he restrained himself. Why were they trying to keep this a secret from him? He knew in his gut that Larry had lied to him about the noise he had heard.

TV, my ass. And about nature suddenly calling. More like a guilty conscience.

And then the thought hit him. *If Rachel is at Larry's house right now, considering that this town is about to be attacked again by a major snow event, is Rachel planning to stay the night? And would it be the first time?*

"Oh, my God," he said out loud.

He didn't think Larry would be wrong for his twin sister. It was just the opposite. Randall knew no better man in the world than Larry Carter. Nice, great sense of humor, caring, law-abiding. Randall knew Larry would be the best thing to happen to Rachel Arthur. The problem was that for all his life, Randall had assumed that Larry had thought of Rachel as a sister, in the same way that sibling-less Larry thought of Randall as a brother. Randall had always assumed that Rachel had nothing but sisterly feelings for Larry—if even that. Now, that lifetime assumption was out the window. But why were they keeping it so hush-hush? They were probably afraid he would react just like he was in his mind.

No longer able to concentrate on his work, Randall saved

the material he had composed into the laptop computer's memory and shut it down for the night, a night soon filled with rapidly falling windswept snowflakes, piling up inch by inch. *Rachel and Larry*, he thought. *Damn.* He had to talk with them soon and get the truth, no matter how much they might resist speaking the truth, before he went nuts pondering the situation.

Chapter Six

ANOTHER NIGHT, ANOTHER MOTEL. THIS ONE WAS THE Baymont Inn and Suites in Topeka, Kansas. Jay had signed in this time as "Steve Bishop." He had made good time driving on the interstate today, with one stop in Colorado Springs to eat at a Wendy's. It was now nearly ten in the evening, and he was just out of the shower and in his underwear briefs, propped up in bed, watching CNN.

The shit was beginning to hit the fan.

The bodies of Connie Shidler and her sister Stephanie Winslow were discovered late last evening, about the time Jay was getting off the interstate in Albuquerque to get to his first motel, by Stephanie's husband, Erik. After repeated unanswered calls to Stephanie's cell phone, then Connie's cell phone, and finally Jay's cell phone (which Jay noticed with a sick smile), Erik went to Jay and Connie's house to see if they were there and hopefully ease his ever-rising panic.

He failed in the latter. Big time.

He walked into the unlocked house and smelled the sick stench of death in the living room immediately. He slowly walked to the couch, saw the shot-up television on the wall, and then saw the bodies of his wife and sister-in-law on the bloodstained, brain-mattered couch. It took him maybe a minute or two to register this nightmarish sight in his brain and to recover his senses enough to call 9-1-1. The police were there in ten minutes. Erik saw the letter between the bodies on the couch but avoided touching it. Some part of his fractured mind could realize sensibly that nothing should be touched until the police arrived; that this was officially a crime scene. So, once he called 9-1-1 on his cell, he walked outside, closed the front door on the tableau of madness inside, sat on the edge of the concrete front porch, waited for the police, and cried his heart out.

Jay was watching the CNN report now, and because of the strange nature of the letter the police had opened (having to find an Arabic translator from nearby Northern Arizona University to read it), it was mentioned. Anything that might relate to Islam, violence, and terrorism on home soil was a sure-fire, bona fide ratings grabber.

The staged video from Jay and Roger had gone viral a few hours ago, first on YouTube, and now on the twenty-four-hour television news channels, surely placing more fear inside the hearts of every American who had watched it, leaving them wondering what in the hell this world was coming to. There would be sadness for the two women murdered by these animals from a foreign country, who spoke a strange tongue, who worshiped a God not connected to Jesus Christ, and who hated us for our freedom and prosperity. There would be not only sadness but also fear for Jay Shidler, who appeared to be fated for execution by these same bastards.

All those people would be rather shocked at the truth of

the situation and would also be shocked at the life he had lived up to now.

Jay Shidler had spent nearly the last ten years being paid to kill people. First, by the United States government, as one of their brave soldiers fighting the Taliban and al-Qaeda in Afghanistan in a war started on a late summer day in 2001, a day when the world truly seemed to go to Hell. He served with distinction in the Army's Special Forces, taking out terrorist and guerilla cells in the rugged and tricky mountains of a country with a long, complicated, and violent history.

His recruiters knew of the skills he already possessed, skills he had first learned as a teenager. He had been fascinated with martial arts since watching movies on television starring people like Chuck Norris, Steven Segal, and even Bruce Lee. He wanted to take karate and other martial arts classes, and his parents were wealthy enough and loved him enough to allow him to follow his youthful desires.

His dad hired the best instructors, first in basic karate and then in judo and kung fu. Jay's dad had even bought him DVD sets of the TV series *Kung Fu* with David Carradine. By the time Jay graduated from his private high school with honors, he had high-degree black belts in karate, judo, and kung fu. Trophies lined two shelves in his bedroom, not unlike a particular person in the city Jay was traveling toward now—a person who was now a college professor/private investigator. Jay attended college, majoring in business administration, hoping to take over from his father when he decided to pass the torch from father to son. And Jay would consider his expertise in multiple martial arts a sideline, a fun hobby.

However, when he was just twenty years old and about to begin his sophomore year at SUNY Buffalo, he fell out with his father. With the nation still angry over the events of September 11, 2001, and now in wars of revenge in Afghanistan and soon to be in Iraq, he left school. He abandoned the assured future of controlling his father's lucrative business to be a killer, not only sharpening his skills in inflicting violence with his hands and feet but also to learn new ways to kill. Simpler ways involving mechanical weapons. He took the chance when given it in 2002 and never looked back.

After six years, he grew tired of the controlled rigors of the military and saw an opportunity to take his talents into the private sector. He left the service in 2008 with the rank of captain and quietly put the word out to certain underground sources that he could offer those talents to those who needed problems solved quietly but firmly. That availability would not be inexpensive. Even though he liked the AC/DC song, Jay did not believe in Dirty Deeds, Done Dirt Cheap. He demanded what he truly believed his talents to be worth, and those needing those particular solutions did not mind paying that price, the same way his father had not minded paying highly for his instruction. He accepted jobs in Asia, Europe, Africa, and even the United States. He performed his tasks as part of a mercenary team, which offered him more flexibility than the U.S. Army, or as a solo assassin, taking care of business with no evidence left behind except a dead body or two. Sometimes more.

Jay saw enough of the reporting, turned off the television with the remote, turned out the lights, and was asleep in less than ten minutes. Jay Shidler felt as if he were as close to a finely tuned machine as any human being could be. That made him feel no guilt over the people he'd killed but pure pride. However, that was a pride he had to keep tampered down to live within the shadow world of assassins. It seemed to Jay sometimes that he had lived in the shadow world all his life, even before the split with his father and his destiny after that.

Chapter 7

Thursday

Eleven inches of snow.

Eleven inches of snow in eight hours.

Plus, the ten inches on the ground already.

Put simply, it was a goddamn mess.

Randall was awakened at six-thirty by his phone alarm and saw a text from FCC saying that classes had been canceled for today and Friday. This text had gone out to all staff and students. He got out of bed, showered, bundled up, shoveled the front porch of snow, and cleared a path to the driveway. Then he cleared away as much snow as he could from his car. It was a pain in the ass, as it always was, but he got the chore done and was glad to get back into the warm confines of the house.

Around ten o'clock, Randall went upstairs to his PI office to start work on the Bryan Bowles case. After looking up the number on his phone directory app, Randall called Burt Olivetti. He introduced himself by name only. "I didn't know whether you'd be at your office or home because of all the snow. I hope I'm not intruding."

"No, it's not a problem at all, Mr. Arthur. Since my one court appointment got canceled and I had no appointments at the office today, I planned on sticking around with the family. So, what can I do for you on this miserable morning?"

"I'm a private investigator here in Falcon City. Bryan Bowles has hired me concerning the DVD you recorded of his father in your office before his stroke."

"Oh, yes. I'm not surprised to be getting a call like this. I assumed Bryan would hire someone to help him discover what his father was trying to tell him on that recording that I made for him. I don't know how much help I will be to you, but I can tell you what I know."

"Well, first of all, what did Joseph Bowles tell you regarding why he approached you instead of the family lawyer?"

"He told me he didn't want the Bowles' attorney to have a conflict of interest since he represents Roger. He didn't wish for Roger to know what he was doing."

"Do you know Mr. Holbrook, the Bowles' attorney?"

"Indeed, I do. By the way, are you related to Rachel Arthur, the attorney?"

"She's my twin sister."

"Oh, is that right? She's a nice lady. Damn talented lawyer, too."

"Thank you." Randall smiled to himself. "I agree with you on that."

"Back to Mr. Holbrook. I do know him, and he contacted me after Joseph Bowles' death when he discovered he was in my office. It was then that I had to do something that I did not enjoy doing. I had to lie to him."

"About why Joseph was there in the first place."

"Yes. I couldn't tell him about the DVD, having been instructed before the actual recording of the disc by Mr. Bowles not to tell anyone except Bryan. I told Mr. Holbrook that he suffered his stroke before he could tell me the reason for his visit."

"Did he buy it?"

"I assume he did. But my lie left him no answers to his, and I would guess the family's questions about why Joseph Bowles came to see an outside attorney. Do you know Paul Holbrook, Mr. Arthur?"

"By name only." Before Bryan left the house yesterday, Randall had asked him if the Mr. Holbrook that his father had spoken of on the recording was Paul Holbrook, and Bryan said it was. The name brought back memories of not so long ago.

Last spring, Paul Holbrook's teenage son, Jack, was discovered dead in his bedroom by his parents. He had died taking pills that were filled with heroin, with the street name Burmese Blue. That event ended up being connected to Randall's first case as a PI which eventually sent him across the country and the Pacific Ocean to Australia and had a not-so-happy ending. What he was told by his police detective friend, Joe Kayla, about Jack's parents' reaction to their son's death was that they weren't so much grief-stricken as embarrassed by the way their son met his end. That a drug-related death for their only child was not befitting such a family in high standing. Randall wasn't surprised that someone with the mentality of Paul Holbrook was the attorney for a privileged family like the Bowles.

"How did Mr. Bowles seem to you when he entered your office? On the recording, he didn't look that well."

"He didn't look that well in person. He looked not only sick but...well, very despondent. I asked him if he was okay. He said no; he was anything but okay. Those were his exact words."

"Whose recorder did you use for the recording?"

"Mine. He called me to set up the appointment and said he wished me to record something for his son, Bryan. It was already set up by the time he arrived."

"And he never told you before the recording what he would say?"

"No, sir. I was to find out when he said it during the recording. But he never got far enough to fully answer the question of why he was recording it."

"How long was it after you called 9-1-1 that help arrived?"

"About five minutes. My office building isn't far from the hospital."

"You said Mr. Holbrook asked you why Joseph came to you instead of him. Did Roger contact you, as well?"

"Roger called me not long after Mr. Holbrook talked to me and asked me the same questions."

"What was his demeanor? How persistent was he in his questioning?"

"He was persistent, to a point. But when he gleaned that I knew very little about the purpose of his father's visit because of the timing of his stroke, he seemed satisfied. We said our goodbyes and hung up. Haven't heard from anyone from the family, or their lawyer, since then. I'm sorry I can't tell you more, Mr. Arthur."

"I understand. You've been gracious to tell me what you have."

"If I can help in the future, please feel free to call."

"Thank you. How much help would Mr. Holbrook be if I questioned him?"

Olivetti laughed. "Not very much. He's not going to give up any family secrets that he might be privy to, especially to a private investigator hired by the black sheep son. No offense to either you or Bryan."

"None taken. I'll give it a shot, anyway. Sometimes, what someone doesn't tell you tells you a lot. You lawyers should know that by now."

"Indeed. Good luck, Mr. Arthur."

"Thanks. If you do have to get out in this mess, be careful."

"I will. You do the same. Goodbye."

"Bye." Randall disconnected. Okay, so he didn't know much more than he did before calling Olivetti. Joseph Bowles had discovered something upsetting enough about his oldest son that he felt compelled to contact an attorney outside his own and record a message for his estranged son. But he hadn't held out long enough physically to tell either Bryan or Olivetti what the issue was. So, what now? Randall figured there was so much data about nearly anything on the Internet that there must be something on the affluent Bowles family of Falcon City, New York.

Deciding to take a break from the Bowles case, Randall went downstairs to work on his book for a bit. He would tackle this mystery dropped on his snowy doorstep later.

Chapter Eight

As Randall was typing in his downstairs office, he realized that neither Larry nor Rachel had called him yet. Had they been too busy? And if so, with what? Randall was afraid to answer that question, but he took the initiative and called Larry instead.

Larry's cell rang several times before his voicemail responded. One can tell a lot about a person from their voicemail or answering machine message, and one could tell from listening to Larry Carter's message that he was still a kid at heart despite closing in on middle age. The message went like this: "Hello. You have reached Elmer J. Fudd, millionaire. I own a mansion and a yacht. Just kidding. This is Larry Carter. I'm not available right now to return your call, so please leave your name, number, and message after the annoying beep, and I'll get back to you as soon as possible." Then, the annoying beep.

"Hey, Larry. It's me. Just calling to chat. Hope you're not out in this mess when you don't have to be. Call back when you get a chance. Bye." He hung up. Where in the hell could he be? There wasn't school today, so he couldn't be there. Maybe he had to run an errand.

Or maybe he's somewhere with Rachel.

Randall waited about fifteen minutes, resuming working on his laptop. Then he called Rachel. Her cell rang twice before she answered.

"Hello."

"Hey, sis."

"Hey, yourself. Survived another Falcon City blizzard, we did."

"Yeah."

"I actually just got back home."

"Oh? Where've you been?"

There was a brief silence on the line. "Promise me you won't freak out."

"Why would I freak out?"

"Just promise, okay?"

Randall knew what was coming. "Okay, I promise I won't freak out."

"I spent the night with someone."

"You were at Larry's house last night, weren't you?"

Randall heard a low moan at the other end. "How did you know?"

"When Larry called me last night, I could hear you clear your throat in the background. I know that sound anywhere."

"You'd make a good private eye."

"Yeah," Randall replied in a sarcastic tone. "I might have to try starting my own part-time business sometime."

"Very funny. Look, Randy, I can explain."

"You don't owe me an explanation. You're a big girl; it's

your life. What you do and who you do it with is not my business."

"It is when it's with your best friend."

"I just don't understand why Larry lied to me and told me that no one was there with him."

"I know. After he did it, we both realized that it was stupid. It was stupid not to tell you what's been happening with us lately. We were just afraid of what your reaction would be."

"What did you think I was going to do, beat Larry up for being with my sister? Larry's one of the best people I've ever known. You could do a hell of a lot worse than him. And have, in the past. But you got it right this time. I just always assumed that you and he thought of each other as more brother and sister or just pals."

"Well, until recently, we thought that, too. But something funny happened along the way."

"Guess so."

"Look, I'm sorry we kept you in the dark about this. But this took us by such a surprise that we didn't know how to react to it, as far as you were concerned. Listen, I want to explain this further to you, but I would rather do it face-to-face with you than over the phone. Is that okay with you?"

"Yeah, of course it is."

"They should have the streets cleared enough by tonight to drive on them without many problems. Why don't you, Larry, and I get together here at my place tonight if we can? I'll fix a great dinner, and the three of us can discuss this and clear up any misunderstandings."

"I'd like that."

"Seven o'clock?"

"I'll do my best to be there."

"Are we okay?"

"We're more than okay, babe."

"Are you and Larry okay?"

"Yeah, Larry and I are okay, too. By the way, I tried to call him not long ago but got his voicemail. And you might want to tell him that the Elmer J. Fudd reference on his voicemail is getting old."

Rachel laughed. "He's honestly thinking about changing it to saying he's Wile E. Coyote, genius."

"Good lord."

"Anyway, to answer your question, he followed me home to ensure I made it back safely. He left a few minutes ago."

"I left a message, so he should call back soon."

"In that case, I'll go. Talk to you later."

"All right."

"Randy?"

"Yeah?"

"I'm sorry."

"I know. Me, too."

"I love you."

"I love you, too."

"Do you still love Larry?"

"If he goes ahead with that Wile E. Coyote message, I might have to stop. But for now, yeah, I still love Larry, too."

"Cool. Bye."

"Bye." So, that mystery was solved, even though he still had to find out more. Like, how in the heck did this happen? But that was something for tonight. A minute after disconnecting with Rachel, the phone rang. He saw on the caller ID that it was indeed Larry.

"Hello, Larry."

"Hey, Randy. Enjoying the snow?"

"Hell no."

"Me, either."

"I know, Larry."

"You know what?"

"I know that Rachel spent the night with you last night. I just talked to her. She ratted you guys out."

"Shit. The girl doesn't like having a guilty conscience."

"She's a lawyer. You know how they feel about the concept of the truth."

"Yeah. Are you mad at me?"

"That you and my sister are seeing each other? No. Shocked? Definitely. I'm just hurt you lied to me about her not being there last night."

"I'm sorry, bud. I freaked out and did the first thing that occurred to me. Lie. We should have told you sooner."

"Look, forget all that. What's done is done. Rachel and I have already had this discussion. She's inviting us to her house tonight for dinner, weather permitting, so we can talk more about this in person."

"Sounds like a plan."

"So, if you're wondering, there's no problem with you and I, or myself and my sister. So, let's gobble down Rachel's delicious cooking tonight and get this all straight and clear. What do you say?"

"I say, let's do it!"

"Hey, Larry?"

"Yeah?"

"The Elmer Fudd reference on the voicemail is getting old."

"I'm thinking about changing it to saying that I'm Wile E. Coyote, genius."

"Yeah, Rachel told me. Larry, do you remember what happened to Wile E. Coyote in that cartoon when he bragged about being a genius to Bugs Bunny? And then later, when he just had to notch it up to 'super genius'?"

"I recall that Bugs Bunny ended up kicking Wile E.'s brown coyote ass."

"Bingo."

"Your point being?"

"If you're going to say that you're one of the Looney Tunes characters, always go with Bugs. Or perhaps the Road Runner. Always go with a winner, Larry—beep, beep. Now, there are two annoying beeps for you. Have a nice evening." Before Larry could say anything, Randall pressed the disconnect icon on the phone and smiled.

Chapter Nine

Randall was finished working on the Great Lakes shipping book for the day. It was 5:45 P.M. The local news was dominated by the snowstorm. The city was not as paralyzed as it had been last night and this morning, but there were still a lot of cancellations. FCC was off again tomorrow, as were Falcon City High, Boone County High, and other schools in the area.

The Boone County schools had the issue of having their students living in the rural section of the county that spread south of Falcon City, and most of the rural roads were tougher for the road crews to reach more immediately. Thankfully, the streets within Falcon City were clear enough that people could travel relatively safely this evening. Sadly, there had still been several fender-benders and more serious accidents that had cost a couple of people their lives. It was almost always the case when one of these blizzards struck. Somebody would be foolish enough to travel within the tumult of the storm, and the storm would nearly always prevail. A storm like that had just hit rarely showed mercy in either the thick or the aftermath of its release.

Randall had moved from one office to another, now upstairs in his PI lair. He would go to his sister's house in an hour for dinner with her and Larry. He hoped it wouldn't be awkward now that he knew of their romantic situation. He would try his best not to make it so. He was sitting at his computer for the moment, doing what not only any good private investigator but any citizen would do if they wanted information about someone in this technologically ruled age—he was googling. The first subject he typed into the search engine was "Bowles family, *Falcon City Expression*." Within seconds, he got hundreds of hits. He was presently looking for the basics; some facts he already knew and just wanted to refresh his memory, and maybe some things he didn't know.

The first place he went to was the *Falcon City Expression* website itself. From what he had been hearing lately, the website was read more than the actual physical newspaper by the Falcon City faithful. It was that way with most newspapers in large and small cities. Physical newspapers were slowly becoming as rare as an ethical politician. Publishers had to accept this new reality and, like REO Speedwagon once sang, "roll with the changes."

Word was that Roger Bowles was gradually moving the *Expression* to a exclusively digital edition, reducing the number of papers printed for sale in increments and that in a few years, the actual physical newspaper, with its ink that had the annoying habit of rubbing off onto the skin of one's fingers, which was tossed by kids onto front lawns and placed into vending machines and onto store shelves would be forever gone. Randall figured it was just a sign of the times, like many other things, but he found the idea of no more physical newspapers sad.

Maybe he was just an old fogey, even though he was still in his thirties, but he was a history professor who had a love for the past, and even though he wasn't exactly a Luddite, he thought some traditions were nice to keep around, just to remind people of the way the world used to be. Just because society was becoming more high-tech, that did not mean it was improving in all things, like common courtesy, civility, and an understanding of the past and why that was important. He thought people were caring less for each other overall and were becoming too self-absorbed. He thought the true "Me Generation" was not in the 1970s but right here, right now, as another band called Jesus Jones once sang.

The website itself didn't give out much personal information about the Bowles family, except for a touching 2003 tribute written by Joseph Bowles about his wife, who had just committed suicide. It displayed that the paper had existed since 1903, albeit in small letters, printed just below the *Expression* masthead. Randall didn't need to look on Google, Bing, or any other strangely titled search engine to know that it was Joseph Bowles' grandfather, Edward Bowles, who had founded the newspaper back when Teddy Roosevelt was president and the debut of an event called the World Series was just months in the future. It had passed on to Joseph's father, Zachary Bowles, then to Joseph, and now to Roger. What was on the website presently mainly was news about the death of Joseph Bowles and the blizzard—news that he had garnered from the television news earlier. The meteorological divisions of the *Expression* and the local TV and radio stations must have a field day every winter, living in a city on the shores of Lake Ontario, the constant bitch for lake-effect storms.

Randall logged off the *Expression* website and went to Wikipedia to see what he could find. There were articles about the paper and its history, but they were all facts Randall already knew. Sadly, nothing would lead him to figure out why Joseph Bowles would desperately attempt to contact his estranged son. There was no dirt at all, just facts meant for public knowledge. He found several journalism awards over the years—no Pulitzers, but mostly from New York State, both in news and sports coverage. Its news organization was respected in the state and the Northeastern United States. Something that deserved a self-feeling of pride. There was mention of a tragic car accident outside Buffalo in 1982 that claimed the lives of two *Expression* reporters, but from reading the actual accounts, that just seemed to be a cruel twist of luck and nothing criminal.

He then went from the newspaper family to the black sheep of the family. He googled Bryan's name and immediately got hits about the *Family Dynamics* strip. The Wikipedia article on Bryan himself was relatively short. Nothing about the estrangement from his family, just that he attended Syracuse University and took a home-study course in cartooning. He had married just out of college to someone he met there, and they had two small daughters, all of whom Randall had seen at the hockey game. He had syndicated *Family Dynamics* in 2008, and it appeared in roughly eight hundred newspapers, not only in the United States but also in several countries worldwide, and on the Internet. As expected, it didn't mention that one newspaper that did not carry the strip was the *Falcon City Expression*.

Randall logged off the computer, satisfied that he had learned as much as he could for the moment. He picked up his cell, looked up Bryan's number which he had added to his contact list yesterday, and called him. A woman answered, Randall assuming it was the wife.

"Hello, is this Mrs. Bowles?"

"Yes, this is Emily Bowles. May I ask who's calling?"

"This is Randall Arthur, Emily. If Bryan is free, I'd like to speak to him briefly, if I could."

"Oh, certainly, Mr. Arthur," she replied, almost with what Randall could pick up as a jovial response. "Hold on, just one moment, please, and I'll get him for you."

"Thanks." He just had to wait about twenty seconds before Bryan's voice came on the other end. "Hey, Randy. What's going on?"

"Not much in this weather."

Bryan laughed. "Tell me about it."

"I was wondering how long it usually takes the county road crews to clear the area around your home so you can get in and out?"

"They're pretty good at clearing the road and the driveway up to the house. I'm sure the city itself gets priority, but they have enough of a crew to work in the rural areas simultaneously, though sometimes it takes more time out on the rural roads. Although my home is just off the main highway and not on a rural road, they usually get to me quickly. Why do you ask?"

"I wanted to come out and visit. Talk about your experiences with your family, both during the good and bad times, if that's okay. Any information I can learn might help me."

"Well, there wasn't as much good as bad, but sure, we'd love to have you come on over when you get a chance."

"Great. I was planning on calling your brother this evening to set up a meeting with him sometime tomorrow. Maybe I could come by after that and tell you how that went."

"Sounds good. I'll be here, drawing my funny pictures."

Randall laughed. "And making lots of money doing so."

"Not jealous, are you?"

"Very." They both laughed.

"I don't think that you're going to get much information out of Roger, that is if he even agrees to see you."

"Oh, I know that. And I think I can persuade him to see me. I have special private detective talents at my disposal."

"That's what I was hoping for when I hired you."

"I'll give you a heads-up after I talk to him and let you know when I'll be at the house."

"Sounds good. Let me tell you how to get here." Bryan gave Randall directions. Randall believed the roads would be easy enough if they were passable.

"You and the family have a good rest of the evening. Stay warm."

"You, too. Hey, thanks again for everything. I truly appreciate it."

"I haven't done anything yet so the gratitude might be premature. Hopefully, we'll be on our way to finding out what's happening tomorrow. Talk to you then."

"Okay. Goodnight." Randall disconnected. He got ready to call Roger Bowles. According to what he had heard, there would be no funeral service. Joseph's remains were cremated per his wishes, and there would be a memorial service later, but it had not been scheduled yet. So, there would be no immediate funeral plans Randall would intrude upon if he called now.

However, the family was still in mourning. It might hamper his ability to interview Roger as quickly as he'd like. He took the shot anyway. He quickly looked up Roger's number on the directory app and dialed. This time, he got who he was looking for on the first try.

"Hello."

"Mr. Bowles?"

"Yes, this is Roger Bowles."

"Hello, sir. My name is Randall Arthur. First, my condolences to you and your family on your father's passing. I know this is probably not the greatest timing in the world for you, but something has come to my attention that I think you need to know about."

"Thank you for your condolences, Mr. Arthur. And you're right; it isn't the best timing in the world. What is so important that you would call me during our mourning?"

"Well, sir, I am a private investigator, and I have been hired by your brother, Bryan, to investigate something left for him by your father before he passed away. I hoped you could help me find out more about it."

"Mr. Arthur, if indeed my brother hired you, he has already explained that he is no longer a part of this family. My father disowned him years ago, and so have I. Why would my father want to contact Bryan?"

"Well, sir, I was hoping to meet with you sometime in the morning to explain what is going on fully. I don't feel it's the proper place to speak about it over the phone. Would you be willing to meet with me? Place of your choice."

There was silence on the other end for a few moments.

"Will tomorrow morning at ten in my office at the *Expression* building be all right for you?"

"That would be more than all right."

"Fine. I'll see you then. I hope this is worth both of our troubles."

"So do I, sir. Have a good evening, and again, my condolences."

"Thank you. Good night." Roger brusquely disconnected the call before Randall could. "Okay," he said out loud in the empty office. Roger sounded like he thought whatever this visit was going to be about was irrelevant. However, Randall had a surprise for Roger Bowles. Those private investigative talents he mentioned to Bryan would be in play tomorrow, and it would be interesting to see where they ultimately led.

He got up and left the PI office, ready to leave his place for Rachel's and a late dinner with his sister and best friend, now a couple. *Damn*, he thought.

When Roger ended the call, sitting in his living room recliner still dressed in his suit and tie he'd worn most of the day, he allowed himself to panic even more than when he was listening to Randall Arthur over the phone, not wanting the PI to hear even the slightest trace of nervousness in his replies. But now, at least inwardly, he held nothing back.

You son of a bitch. Even when you're dead, you're trying to stop this from happening! Well, you're going to lose. This is happening, no matter what! And I will get what is rightfully mine!

Chapter Ten

When Randall arrived at Rachel's house a little after seven, Larry was already there, relaxing on the living room couch, watching a college basketball game on one of the ESPN networks. "Hey, Randy," he said as Randall handed his just disrobed coat to Rachel to hang up and entered the room from the foyer.

"Hey. What's up, doc?"

"Haha. Definitely not the temperature. Colder than a Stanley Kubrick movie out there." Randall sat down next to Larry on the couch as he was chuckling at Larry's highbrow joke. Rachel said, "You guys hang out for a few minutes while I get everything ready in the dining room."

"No problem," said Randall. As Rachel left the living room, he asked Larry, "So, who's playing and who's winning?" The broadcast has just gone to a commercial break.

"Georgia and Kentucky, from Rupp Arena. Kentucky's up by five early in the first half."

"I remember when Kentucky's players actually stayed for more than one season. How about you?"

"Yeah, I seem to recall that, too. Since Calipari took over, all that program seems to be is a one-and-done grooming year for the NBA. It's like fucking *Dancing with the Stars*—different cast each season."

"And the sad thing is most of these kids, talented as they may be, will get their millions, and end up with a short career, and be out of the game before they know what hit them. I just hope they're smart enough to finish their studies or hire a good financial manager."

"I agree. But I don't see this new reality ending anytime soon. I mean, if you were a young kid offered millions of dollars, wouldn't you be tempted?"

"Of course. And you would, too."

"Damn right."

They both laughed as the game resumed. "You sure we're good, Randy?"

"We be good, pal." Randall held out a fist for Larry to knock with a fist bump, which he did. "But keep in mind that the brother of the girl you're dating has several black belts, if you know what I mean." He winked at Larry.

"Wouldn't think of forgetting, my friend."

"I can't think of anyone better who I'd want dating my sis. I just wish you guys had been less secretive with me about it. I wouldn't have freaked out...well, not too much."

"Neither Rachel nor I were thinking straight on that one, I must admit. We just both love you so much and needed you to be okay with us, you know...being a couple. I know it's going to be something new to get used to. It's a little weird for us, too."

"I'm sure. It's all good, I promise."

Rachel came out of the dining room. "Okay, guys, dinner is ready. Get your asses in here and eat."

"You could be a little more polite," Randall said, winking and smiling at Larry, who smiled back.

"You could shut your mouth and obey your twin sister."

Randall looked at Larry. "Does she talk like that to you?"

"All the time."

"Must be the lawyer in her." Another laugh between the two buddies on the couch.

"In here, now! Both of you!"

"Okay, okay," said Randall as he and Larry rose off the couch, Larry turning off the game with the remote as he did so.

They entered the dining room, just off the kitchen, similar to the layout of Randall's house. Three plates were already set out on the table, with roast beef, mashed potatoes, corn, and green beans servings. Next to them sat glasses of iced sweet tea. They sat down and began eating.

"So," Rachel asked Randall between bites of her food, "anything new going on in your PI biz?"

"Yeah, as a matter of fact, I just got a new case. Believe it or not, I've been hired by Joseph Bowles' estranged son, Bryan." Randall had not previously mentioned meeting Bryan between periods of the hockey game the other night to either Larry or Rachel, not knowing whether their initial meeting in Randall's office would pan out to a hired job.

"Wait, do you mean the dude that draws that comic strip, *Family Dynamics*?" asked Larry.

"That would be the dude."

"I didn't even know they were estranged," said Rachel. "What's going on?"

Randall told them the story of Joseph's final recorded message to Bryan and what happened while recording it.

"Damn," said Larry. "I heard that he'd had a stroke in his lawyer's office. But it sounds more intriguing than anyone really knew."

"Well, here's where it gets a little more interesting. The lawyer he was seeing was Burt Olivetti. However, he's not the family attorney." Randall looked over at Rachel. "Guess who the regular attorney is. I'll give you a hint—he shares an office building with you."

Rachel knew immediately whom Randall meant. "Paul Holbrook," she said with a hint of disdain. She and Holbrook had offices in the same building downtown. She did not like him at all. Thankfully, the times that they saw each other within the confines of the building were infrequent, their offices being on different floors. "I recall seeing both Joseph and Roger Bowles coming into the building occasionally, going up to Paul's office, so I knew he was their attorney. But why would Joseph go to another lawyer?"

"To keep Roger from finding out. He even said that on the recording."

"But Roger probably already knows he was in Olivetti's office when he had the stroke," said Larry.

"Yeah. He's already called Olivetti about it. He didn't tell Roger the truth about why Joseph was there."

"Burt is bound by client confidentiality not to tell Roger anything," said Rachel.

"Exactly. Which would drive Roger nuts."

"Have you talked to Roger yet?" asked Larry.

"I have a meeting with him in his office at ten tomorrow morning."

"That should be rather interesting."

"He's not going to tell you a lot," said Rachel, "if he is indeed hiding something."

"Oh, I know. But sometimes you can learn a lot by what someone doesn't tell you, or what you tell them, and their reaction to that."

Rachel gave her brother one of the stern looks Randall had seen much of over the years, as had Larry more recently. "You have something planned, don't you?"

Randall smiled at his twin sister and best pal, both now a dating couple, something Randall found himself growing steadily more comfortable accepting. He told them what he hoped to achieve at tomorrow's meeting.

When he had finished detailing his plan to them, both Rachel and Larry stared at him, Larry slowly shaking his head. "I think you might be asking for trouble, my friend."

Randall smiled. "Trouble is my middle name," he said in fake bravado.

"No, it isn't, Randall *Lorenzo* Arthur," said Rachel, in her sternest sisterly tone. "I hope you know what you're doing. Please, be careful."

"Don't you guys worry. I can take care of myself. All will be well."

Those words would haunt all three people sitting at that table, beginning approximately forty-eight hours later.

Chapter Eleven

Jay was driving on Interstate 70, thirty miles east of Columbia, Missouri, and approximately ninety miles west of St. Louis, when the tightly scheduled plan conceived by him and Roger Bowles began to unravel somewhat.

Ten miles ahead of his current location, there had been an accident involving five automobiles and one semi-trailer. One car followed too closely to the semi when the semi slowed for traffic ahead of it. The woman driving the car was looking down at a text on her cell phone while driving at nearly eighty miles per hour, and when she looked up from the phone, she didn't have time to register that the truck ahead had slowed. She was still going fast, and she rammed into the rear of the trailer head-on, killing her instantly. The impact from behind forced the semi off the road, and the four cars immediately behind the ill-fated woman were drawn into the melee, crashing into the mess ahead. Two were killed, four injured, and the rest walked away physically unscathed, but shaken mentally. Regrettably, the other cars had crossed into the passing lane and ended up blocking traffic in both lanes.

Jay came upon the traffic jam caused by the accident and cursed out loud in the privacy of his car. He knew immediately what was going on ahead of him, and he realized he would not make it to Columbus, Ohio, as originally planned this evening for his overnight motel stay and would have to figure out a new place to go, not as far as Columbus, forcing the timing of his arrival in Falcon City to be delayed.

While he was not moving in the traffic jam, he took out his cell, activated his version of the DARPA-devised phone-scrambling app he had given Roger, and called him to tell him what was happening. After Roger's curse or two on the other end, he was silent for a moment. He told Jay to hold on while he checked out something. Roger then used the web on his iPhone to search for motels ahead of Jay's current position, where he might spend the night instead of Columbus. He finally told Jay to continue on I-70, once clear of the traffic blockage, to St. Louis and drive across southern Illinois into Indiana. He was then instructed to stop in Indianapolis, where there was a Motel 6 one and a half miles off the interstate where he could spend the night. He told Jay he would call the motel to see if they had any vacancies, and if they did, he would arrange for him to stay overnight at the motel. He would call Jay back shortly with the details if all went well with the phone call to the motel.

Jay disconnected from Roger, resigned himself to the fact that he was going to be stuck here for a bit, and took a deep breath or two to keep calm. In his profession, keeping calm in the face of pressure was a necessity.

His mind returned to the last mission he had undertaken before this one. It was five months ago, last August, in the northern Muslim section of Nigeria. There was a fledgling

Islamic terrorist organization called Karfin Allah, which in the Hausa language meant "The Might of Allah," that was making some noise in that part of the world, bombing marketplaces and churches in both the northern Muslim and southern Christian sections of the country. Boko Haram was the major terrorist threat in Nigeria, but the leader of Karfin Allah, Kamal Jaden, thought they were getting out of control, losing the true focus of their mission. They were killing Muslims, along with everyone else, not caring who died as long as Boko Haram was making waves. Jaden was once a member of Boko Haram but left to start his own group, a group he thought could be more effective in bringing Nigeria and the rest of the African continent over to the rule of Islam. Hence the name of the group. When Jay thought of the name "Boko Haram," he couldn't help but think that it sounded so like Procol Harum, the old British rock group that did songs like "Conquistador" and "A Whiter Shade of Pale."

The State Security Service, the Nigerian domestic intelligence arm, was observing this new and deadly group and knew that if it remained unchecked, Nigeria would be in even more dire straits under the terrorists' whim than it currently was. They decided that Karfin Allah was still in its infancy and could be easily removed from the equation without too much blowback. But how? And who would do it?

People within the agency knew of Jay Shidler and his abilities. They put out the covert word that he was wanted for a special mission that would be quite profitable if successful. Once he received that word, he was flown to Nigeria to meet with officials from the agency, who explained what they wanted done. They knew Jaden's movements and where he would be on a particular night. They wanted to make a statement, so Jay was directed not only to kill Jaden but also his entire family. Shidler agreed, but on one condition—if he needed a favor in the future, he could come to them and ask without hesitation in agreeing to whatever he wanted. After some back-and-forth, they agreed. They gave Jay the latest intelligence on where Jaden and his family were located, the property layout, how many guards he had posted outside, and even what time the family turned in for the evening.

Jay deployed with a Nigerian Army company of approximately one hundred soldiers. The company's mission was to take out the main group of terrorists in the city of Bama, while Jay and four handpicked soldiers broke off from the main group and snuck into the Jaden compound. An Army chopper took Jay from the capital of Abuja to the battalion base in Maiduguri, where they would proceed southeast into Bama at the appointed time. Jay spoke not a word of Kausa or Fulani, but a few of the soldiers spoke English, including the company's captain, who was the one who primarily communicated with Jay. Jay ensured the four who went with him to the Jaden compound also spoke English. Jay's orders to his four comrades were simple—kill the guards outside, and I will take care of the family inside the house. And you allow me to take care of business my way. No questions, no arguments.

As the sun was descending toward the horizon in the hazy distance, one of the Nigerian soldiers was sitting with Jay on the steps of the front deck of one of the barrack buildings. "Beautiful sunset, isn't it, sir?" asked the soldier.

"Yeah. This is the first African sunset I've watched. I've watched sunrises and sunsets worldwide, but never here—until now."

"I wonder if Kamal Jaden and his family are also watching the same sunset. If they are, it will be their last."

"Does it bother you that I've been ordered to kill not just Kamal but his wife and children, too?"

The soldier was silent momentarily, watching the sinking sun and contemplating. "Normally, it would. However, this is war. Sometimes in war, to gain victory, there must be, how do you put it... collateral damage?"

"Yeah. Collateral damage," Jay said sarcastically.

Jay and his team of four left the barracks at 2200 hours, simultaneously with the rest of the company heading toward Bama. They traveled first by Jeep for about six miles and then left the vehicle behind a thick clump of bushes by the side of the road to continue on foot toward the Jaden compound. They all wore night-vision goggles, but the four uniformed soldiers carried semi-automatic rifles and silenced pistols. In contrast, Jay carried just his SIG Sauer Mosquito semi-automatic pistol, the same gun that would be used soon to kill his wife and sister-in-law, with spare ammo on his belt. It was still humid, even after the sunset and the arrival of darkness. However, it was more bearable than the earlier daylight when it had reached over one hundred degrees Fahrenheit. The Nigerians were accustomed to this climate; they fought in it day and night without complaint. The last time Jay had operated outdoors in hot climate was in Afghanistan. He didn't miss the heat, but sometimes he missed the camaraderie of his fellow soldiers, the challenge of drawing the enemy out of their convoluted mountainous lairs and taking them out, once and for all.

They arrived at the rear of the Jaden compound at 2225 hours, hidden by more bush, moving with the stealth of hunters out for the kill, not wanting to give any forewarning to their victims. Jay and one of the soldiers were on the right flank, two in the middle, and one on the left. Six guards surrounded the house—two in the back, standing approximately ten feet from one another, and four spread out in a semi-circle in the front yard. The Nigerian soldier on the left flank from his hiding place in the high bushes quickly shot two of the front guards in the head with his silenced weapon, instantly killing them in the space of mere seconds. The two soldiers in the back killed the two sentries there in the same manner. The soldier with Jay, the one he had watched the sunset with, shot the other two guards at the front while Jay hung back in the bushes, awaiting the signal that all the guards were permanently out of the game. The killing of the guards took place within seconds of each other. Not simultaneously, but close enough. Once the soldier on the left flank saw that all were dead, he gave Jay a hand signal, and Jay proceeded up the steps of the house's front porch. He tried the front door and, not to his surprise, found it was locked. He shot the lock with the silenced pistol and went inside while his four Nigerian comrades stood watch outside, near the corpses of the guards.

Jay entered a long hallway that ran down the length of the house to the back door. There were two doors on either side. Jay tried the first door to his left and saw it led to the living room. He then went to the next door on the right, steadily opened it, and found his first two targets. Jaden Kamal and his wife were sound asleep in their bed, both nude, perhaps in the midst of their dreams, unaware that their lives on Earth were about to end. Jay wasted no time in shooting the people, who, to his eyes, were nothing more than colored images through his night-vision goggles. Able to see them well enough to make out their heads, that is where he shot them—Jaden first, wife second. Whatever dreaming they might have been experiencing ended once and for all that night.

Jay wasted no time in going back out into the hallway. He guessed that the children's bedroom was next to their parent's bedroom and tried the next door down the hallway on the right. He was right. Both Kamal boys, one five and the other seven, slept in separate beds on either side of the room. Both wore white pajamas. A normal-thinking human being might have paused or even chosen not to execute such a vile act as killing two innocent children in their sleep, but Jay Shidler was not a normal-thinking human being. He was special. He was a machine that killed without remorse, without guilt. Within seconds, the Kamal brothers were the latest victims of that machine. The kids, although innocent, were not spared the bullet in the head.

Jay came out of the house after the deed was done, only being inside for over a minute and a half. He spoke to the two soldiers in front. "Okay, they're out. Go in and do your business." While Jay waited outside, the two soldiers went in, turned on the lights, took off their goggles, went into the bedrooms, and, with their cell phones, took photos of the dead bodies in their beds, visual evidence to the Nigerian government that the Kamal family was indeed dead. These pictures would be sent to Jay's cell phone shortly, while those who snapped the photos would erase them from their phones. Then they came back out, and all five men quickly left the area, returning the way they had arrived.

While they had been killing a family, the rest of the Nigerian Army company had been killing the majority of

Karfin Allah in Bama, making sure that the burgeoning terrorist organization never truly took root. Jay returned to Abuja, showed his pictures of the dead, and procured his money. He was out of the country hours afterward, back home to Flagstaff and to his wife, who thought he was just out of the country on business for the computer company for whom he worked. That, of course, unbeknownst to her, was just a cover. As was their marriage.

Back in America's heartland on a cold January day, stuck on the interstate, Jay saw that the traffic jam was finally, after about an hour, beginning to make a significant advance forward, the cops and emergency crews having done their work. Roger called back, confirming Jay's overnight reservation at the Indianapolis motel. Jay was in St. Louis by four and across Illinois and into Indianapolis and the Eastern Time Zone by nine. He was in his Motel 6 room and asleep soon after checking in and taking his quick shower. He should be in Falcon City by tomorrow night if nothing else went wrong.

Chapter 12

Friday

"So, Mr. Arthur, why did you want to speak to me this morning?"

Randall was seated in a leather chair on the other side of the desk from Roger Bowles, hands folded on his lap. "Again, let me express my condolences on the passing of your father. I'm sure this has been a terrible time for you and your family. But like I said, a couple of days ago, your brother Bryan asked me to look into something for him. I know he and the rest of your family have been estranged for several years, but he received a DVD from an attorney named Burt Olivetti. Your father, as you probably know, was in his office when he suffered his stroke."

"Yes. I've tried to find out why he was there instead of in the office of our family attorney, but Mr. Olivetti has refused to tell me."

"He can't, Mr. Bowles. If it was a professional visit from your father, Mr. Olivetti is bound by client/attorney confidentiality rules. But I can tell you why he was there."

Roger's eyes widened. "Do tell, Mr. Arthur."

"He was there to record a message to Bryan. He was beginning to tell him you would do something that would destroy the family and that Bryan had to stop it. Sadly, before he could tell him the specifics, he suffered his stroke. What can you tell me of what your father thought you might be doing to destroy the family, Mr. Bowles?"

Roger was quiet for a moment, staring at Randall. "Mr. Arthur, my father, sad to say, was not in his right mind before his death. I would assume that something was going on in his brain that eventually led to his stroke and his rational thinking was beginning to be affected. We thought for a while that he might be beginning to show the early signs of dementia. I assure you, I am planning nothing to harm my family, or Bryan's for that matter. I couldn't care less about my brother's family. As far as I'm concerned, he might as well not exist. He is no longer a member of my family."

"Just because he wanted to be a cartoonist? To follow his dream?"

"Mr. Arthur, this newspaper has been in the Bowles family since the turn of the twentieth century. It will remain in the family throughout this century and hopefully for all time beyond. My children will run the paper after I'm gone. And I assure you, if one or both of them decide to follow their dreams that have nothing to do with our newspaper, they will be disowned as Bryan was. That has been made crystal clear to them, and they will do what is right. It was my father's dream for my brother and I to run the *Expression* together after he retired. He and I could have taken this paper to even greater heights than it is now. But Bryan wanted nothing to do with the business. He wanted to be a fucking 'artist'." Roger made the quotation marks with his fingers when he said that last word. "Bryan was the first member of this family since we started the paper to reject his heritage. And for that, my father, and subsequently the rest of us, made sure he was no longer in this family, except in name."

"Seems very cruel."

"To you, and probably to most other people, it would. But we aren't other people, Mr. Arthur. That's why the paper is what it is today. Despite the hiccup of my brother's abandoning his birthright, this paper will continue to prosper in the twenty-first century digital age."

"I've learned that this paper's circulation has dropped significantly over the last few years, as have most other newspapers. Most people would rather get their news off the Internet these days."

"That's true. And that's why I will eliminate the physical paper version of the newspaper within the next two years. After that, it will be exclusively online. Not only will that increase our readership, but it will also cut the costs of producing the physical paper and the costs of hiring people to deliver those papers. In 1982, when I was just a small child, there was a strike by the union of truck drivers who delivered the newspapers to the sellers and put them in the vending machines. Almost put us out of business. Thankfully, my father was able to negotiate an end to the strike. But it's a digital world now, and I have to adjust to that, just like everyone else."

"What did your father think of this idea to go fully digital?"

"Honestly, he wasn't happy. But you must understand he was old school. He liked the smell and feel of the paper. He enjoyed getting the ink from the paper stained on his fingers."

"Can't blame a man for appreciating the past." Randall left it unsaid that he appreciated it as much as anyone, considering his passion for historical matters.

"I don't. But I also must be realistic about the newspaper business. It's dying. I predict that by 2050, there will be no physical newspapers or magazines. Big city papers like the *New York Times*, *Washington Post*, *Chicago Tribune*, *Sun-Times*, and *Los Angeles Herald-Examiner* will be exclusively online. I'm sure the small-town papers will be the last holdouts, but they'll eventually see the light and follow the winds of change. And although my father was against the idea, since I now run the paper, I have the final say in the paper's operation. So, he learned to accept it. Begrudgingly, I must say, but I think he eventually realized he had to trust my judgment if this paper was to survive. That was the only thing I've done that my father objected to. And I doubt it would destroy the Bowles family. We will just be successfully transitioning with the times. So, I must tell you that whatever was in his mind at the time of that recording to Bryan was a delusion in his decaying mind. The fact that he even made a recording for a son he no longer acknowledged as his is proof that he was not of sound mind. So, Mr. Arthur, please tell my brother and your client that he has nothing to worry about from me. He and his family can live in peace. I have nothing but the best intentions for mine. Tell him that what was recorded on that DVD was the ravings of an old man losing his mind and about to die. Tragic but true. I certainly did not want to see such a great, proud man leave this world in that manner. It especially hurts when it's someone you love. But sometimes life doesn't give you what you want, does it?"

"No, it doesn't."

"If I may ask, where is this DVD now?"

The question Randall had been hoping Roger would ask. "The only copy is in my possession at my home office. Bryan had it, and we watched it together. He had seen enough of it. Since it was so upsetting, he gave it to me in case I could learn anything from it. So far, no luck."

"Well, I'm afraid that you won't find anything. And I'm sure that whatever my father was going to say to Bryan before his stroke hit him would have been delusions in his mind, as I said. Hell, it could have been about my plans to change the paper to only a digital version. He probably came up with some reason why it would ruin the family. He probably thought I would end up bankrupting us or something like that."

"Well, since that is all you can tell me, I guess I'll leave you now. But I am going to keep looking to see what is going on for my client's peace of mind."

"Like I said, you'll be wasting your time."

"Well, it's my time to waste, isn't it?" Randall stood up and grabbed his coat from the back of his chair. He shook hands with Roger across his desk. "Thank you for your time this morning."

"You're welcome. I hope you and Bryan find what you are looking for. Sorry that I couldn't be of more help."

"Have a good day, sir."

"You, too."

As Randall walked out of Roger's office, smiling at his secretary and telling her to have a good day, he thought about what his trained eye saw inside the office—or what he didn't see. There were no pictures at all on Roger's desk, and the ones that hung behind and around him on the oak-paneled wall were of him and his family or him with other important people—the mayor, the governor, several senators, and members of Congress, of him accepting awards on behalf of the *Expression*. Not surprisingly, there were no photos visible of Bryan. To be honest, Randall thought there would be at least one picture of Joseph Bowles.

There were none.

When Randall was out of the office, Roger sat back in his chair, covering his lower face with his right hand. He was frantically thinking of what to do. He took out his cell phone, activated his special app by tapping the triangle, and called Jay Shidler.

Jay answered on the second ring. "Yeah."

"Where are you now?"

"Somewhere in the middle of Ohio. I'm on speaker."

"We have a problem." Roger told Jay of Randall's visit, and of the DVD that was in his possession. "We need to get that DVD and do it now before Arthur figures out what's on it."

"Do you have any ideas on how to do that?"

Roger was quiet for a moment. "Maybe. Let me get off here and make another phone call. I'll get back to you. Safe travels. Get here as soon as you can."

Family Dynamics

"Okay, talk to you soon."

Once Roger disconnected from Jay, he reactivated the scrambler app and dialed another number, this one much closer to home.

The person on the other end answered. "Hello."

"I need a favor."

Chapter Thirteen

Randall knew Roger was hiding something. He could tell by his mannerisms and the look in his eyes during their conversation. He detected hesitancy and nervousness. He knew that Roger's father wasn't just upset over the fact of the *Expression* going digital. A family isn't potentially destroyed over something as trivial as that. He'd planted the seed by telling Roger that the only copy of the DVD was at his house. Now, he would just have to wait and see what, if anything, would grow from that seed. But for now, Randall had called Bryan before leaving the *Expression* office, told him his meeting with Roger was finished, and asked if he could still come over and talk. Bryan said that would be fine.

Randall found the house easily. It was just past the city limits on the state highway between Falcon City and the small town of Simpson's Village. The driveway had been plowed, and he made it up from the highway with no problems. The house was a nice white two-story structure, with an oversized two-car garage, a spacious front yard blanketed in several feet of snow, and a swing set for the kids, which was visible in the backyard, frosted in white.

Seconds after ringing the doorbell, Bryan opened the door. "Hey, Randall. Come on in and take off your coat. It's nice and warm in here, I promise."

"Sounds good to me." Randall removed his thick winter coat and hung it on the coat rack in the foyer.

"Come in and let me introduce you to my family," said Bryan. Randall followed Bryan past a dining room on the right, a table to the left, and then into an expansive living room. Bryan's wife and two little girls were sitting on the couch watching cartoons on the Disney Channel. "Hey, guys, this is Randall Arthur. Randall, my wife, Emily, and our two girls, Becky and Alicia."

"Hello, Randall," said Emily, getting up to shake Randall's hand. "Thank you for helping Bryan out with this."

"No problem. Very nice to meet you." Randall looked at the two girls on the couch. They looked as adorable as they did the other evening at the hockey game. "Hi, girls. Nice to meet you, as well."

"Hi," said Becky.

"Hi," said Alicia. "Nice to meet you, too."

"Randall and I are going into my studio to talk," Bryan told the ladies.

"Okay," said Emily. "Nice meeting you again, Randall."

"Thank you. You, as well." Randall followed Bryan back toward the foyer, where they took a left up the stairs. Bryan led Randall into a large room to the left of the hallway. Bryan's workplace had a loveseat, two chairs, three bookshelves, and art posters—everything from his comic art to drawings by the great Warner Brothers cartoon director

Chuck Jones. The art featured Bugs Bunny, the Road Runner, Wile E. Coyote, and science fiction and fantasy art from the 1970s from artists like Frank Frazetta, Michael Whelan, and Roger Dean. Against the far wall was a large drawing easel and a rolling high-backed leather chair. On the board were a half-finished *Family Dynamics* strip and art pens.

"I didn't interrupt your work, did I?" asked Randall.

"Yeah, but I needed a break. Have a seat." Randall sat in one of the chairs, and Bryan took the other.

"I like your studio. Looks like a nice, comfortable place to work."

"It is. I have everything here I want."

"How far ahead do you draw your strips for the papers?"

"It's four weeks for the dailies and eight for the larger Sunday comics."

"Is it hard coming up with a strip every day?"

"Sometimes. I have days when I'm full of great ideas and others when I struggle to think of something funny. Part of the business, I guess."

"Is the strip still doing well in terms of popularity?"

"Oh, yeah. Last I heard, it was the eighth most popular strip in the country. Believe it or not, I recently received an offer from the Fox network to sell the TV rights so they could make it into an animated series. I'm still mulling it over."

"Wow. They have a good history with animated series. Sounds like a good deal."

"Yeah, maybe. I'm already thinking about going in another direction in my career. I have this idea for a series of graphic novels—what we used to call comic books. It's going to be about a CIA agent who the government brainwashes into

Family Dynamics

becoming a genetically engineered superhero. They're able to keep his CIA training in his mind, plus teach him new skills and enhance him physically so he can run faster, jump higher, have more strength, etc. I have a friend who's a writer. He would write the dialogue, and I'd do all the artwork. It's called *Phenom*."

Randall thought about the idea for a moment. "That sounds like a great story. Would you still draw the strip if you could get this new project off the ground?"

"No. I think I'm getting to a point where I feel like the strip might be getting a little stale. I want to stop it before it gets dull. Get out on top, like Gary Larson did. Maybe I can do the TV deal and get enough money to have my agent sell the graphic novel proposal without worrying about going broke and homeless."

"Well, you'd be disappointing the comic strip fans, but I'm sure they'll want to watch a TV show based on it. As for the graphic novel idea, it sounds like a winner to me. I mean, look at the movies and TV shows these days. You have all these superhero films, and *The Walking Dead* and *Preacher* are hits on TV—both based on graphic novels. I think you might have a potential hit there with your idea."

Bryan smiled. "Yeah, I think so, too. Emily thinks it's a great idea, and my agent thinks it's a great idea. You and I think it's a great idea. The more I think about it, the more I want to go for it. Okay, enough about my future career dreams. What's going on with the case?"

Randall told Bryan of his meeting with Roger and his denial of knowing why his father would say he was threatening the family. He told Bryan of Roger's assertion that Joseph was beginning to lose his mind before the stroke hit him. He also told Bryan about informing Roger that the DVD was in Randall's possession and that there was only one copy.

"You're setting out the bait, seeing if he's going to try to steal it?"

"Yeah. I figure if he's worried enough about what's on the DVD, he'll try to get his hands on it. However, if anyone attempts to break into my house, they will have trouble. I had a break-in last spring where I ended up having to kill the intruder, and I installed an updated security system. Once I set it, anyone trying to get in through the doors or windows will set off a lot of loud noise, which, in turn, will notify the police."

"And I assume you have it set presently."

Randall grinned. "I set it before leaving the house this morning. I have an app on my phone where I can turn it on or off from almost anywhere."

"Have you seen those apps where you get a warning if someone comes to your door while you're away from home?"

"Yeah. They look interesting, but I haven't gotten around to getting one of those yet. Guess I've been too occupied with other things."

Bryan got up and walked over to the window. "Listen, my father and I had our differences, but I don't for a minute believe that bullshit Roger told you about him losing his mind and suddenly spouting weird theories. You and I saw my father on that recording. You and I saw how he looked, how he acted. He didn't look like a crazy man to me. He looked like a very upset man, a *terrified* man. I just can't figure out what in the hell he was trying to tell me. What in the hell is Roger going to do?"

"Listen, hopefully, I've started the process of finding out

the answer to that. And I'm going to watch the DVD again tonight to see if there are any clues, however remote, that I can figure out. Something he said—hell, whatever. But, in the meantime, I would keep a tight watch on your family. Do you have a security system?"

"Yes."

"Good. Make sure you keep it activated and always know the whereabouts of Emily and the girls."

"I'm already paranoid because of all this, so don't worry. I'll take care of them. Emily and I have already discussed several scenarios that might happen and what our response would be. We're ready."

"And I want you to think of anything that your father might have said on that recording, or anything he might have said to you in the past, that might give us an idea of what this is all about. I know it's a long shot, but at least it's a shot."

"I'll do that, too. Hey, while you're here, I want to show you something. Come on over here to the closet. I think you'll get a kick out of this."

"Okay." Intrigued, Randall got up and walked over to the closet. Bryan unfolded the door on its track, got a plastic footstool from inside the closet, and set it out for Randall. "Get up on that and look on the top shelf." Bryan turned on a light that lit the closet's interior.

Randall stepped up on the stool and looked at what was on the top shelf. His eyes widened. Inside a glass case was a nineteenth-century-era telegraph machine. "My God, where did you get this?"

"It was my father's. He bought it at an auction years ago in New York City. He was always fascinated by the history of the telegraph and the life of its inventor, Samuel Morse. I guess it had to do with him being in the newspaper business and all that. It's Civil War-era, according to the people he bought it from. It's been authenticated and everything. Who knows, it could have been used by Grant, Lee, Sherman, or even Abe Lincoln himself. Anyway, he gave it to me for my sixteenth birthday and made me promise I'd take good care of it. That was, of course, before the estrangement. But despite that, I've kept my promise to him. Since you're a history professor, I thought you'd get a kick out of seeing it."

"Yeah. This is freaking cool, indeed!"

"I remember when I was a small kid, my father and I would—"

Bryan was interrupted by Randall's cell phone sounding off in his pants pocket. He stepped off the stool and took the phone out. He saw the caller was Joe Kayla, his friend from the Falcon City Police Department. "Excuse me a moment while I take this."

"Sure."

Randall answered the call. "Hey, Joe. What's up?"

"Where are you right now?"

"At a client's home just outside of town. Why?"

"About twenty minutes ago, a patrol car was near your house, and they saw a young man outside, looking in through the windows, maybe trying to figure out how he could get in. They stopped and approached him, and he started running away from them. He slipped on a patch of snow in a neighbor's yard, and they were able to catch and arrest him. He's here at the station now. You want to come by and see what this is all about?"

"Oh, I already think I know. But, yeah, I'll come over to

the station and fill you in on everything. I want to talk to this guy, too."

"Okay, I'll be here waiting."

"Great. See you soon." Randall disconnected the call.

Bryan looked at Randall. "What's going on?"

"The police caught someone outside my home, possibly looking to break in. The cops have him at the station. I'm going to head over there. Looks like Roger took the bait."

"Hope you can find out something."

"Me, too. Listen, I'll see myself out and let you get back to work. I'll call you later when I find out more, okay?"

"Okay. Talk to you later. Good luck."

"Thanks."

After Randall walked out of the studio, Bryan realized he hadn't been able to finish his story about the telegraph. That got him thinking about something from a long time ago, when Roger, his father, and he were at peace with one another.

Chapter Fourteen

Driving to the police station, Randall had the strange sensation of simultaneously being both pissed off and happy. He was understandably angry that someone had tried to break into his home—twice in the space of a year. But at least now he knew for sure that Roger Bowles did indeed have something he was hiding and planning. He hoped that the man arrested and now at the station would give him some answers, at least enough to lead him on the right path.

It took him about fifteen minutes with traffic to get to the police station in the middle of Falcon City in Government Square, along with the city hall, fire department, and courthouse. In the middle of the square was a fountain that would usually spout its waters but was turned off because of the cold. Randall wondered what it would look like if it were turned on and all the water had frozen in midair. He figured it would indeed be a sight.

He rode the elevator three floors up to the squad room, where Joe Kayla, among other detectives, had his desk. He found him already sitting there, reading what Randall guessed was some sort of report. Joe looked up as Randall approached the desk. "What in the hell have you gotten yourself into this time?"

Randall smiled. "Don't I even get a 'hello'?"

"Sure. Hello. What in the hell have you gotten yourself into this time?"

He sat in the uncomfortable-looking wooden chair in front of Kayla's desk. "What if I told you I think I've pissed off the publisher of the *Falcon City Expression*?"

"You mean Roger Bowles, the son of the one that just died?"

"That'd be the one."

Kayla sighed. "Okay, what's going on?"

Randall told Kayla the whole story, from Bryan Bowles coming up to him in the queue at the Blizzard game to the meeting with Roger this morning. It took a few minutes, and Kayla sat back and patiently listened to his friend. Even though he was a cop, and usually cops and PIs have an antagonistic relationship, Kayla knew Randall long enough. He had been through enough with him to know that if he thought something was worth looking into, it probably was.

"All right," Kayla said when Randall had finished, "you think Roger Bowles hired this guy to break in and steal this DVD? He's probably not going to give him up, you know. And he probably won't be talking without a lawyer present. Someone in Roger's position wouldn't be stupid enough to call him directly and tell him to break into your house. If he had it done, he probably used a middleman."

"I know. I want to see his reaction when I mention Roger's name. Does this guy have a previous record?"

"No, he doesn't, which is weird. His name is Wendell

Shane. He's just eighteen years old. Lives on the west side of town. No record of any type of crime, ever, until today. He's waiting for me to talk to him in the interrogation room."

"May I join you in your interrogation, Detective?"

Kayla sighed. "Sure. Might as well. But you let me do most of the talking since I'm the actual cop here."

"Sure."

"You promise?"

"Cross my heart, hope to die, stick a needle in my eye."

Kayla stared at Randall. "I can't believe that a college professor with a PhD just said something so childish."

"I'm not in college professor mode at the moment. I'm in PI mode. PIs can say childish shit like that."

"Point taken. Follow me."

Randall and Kayla entered the brightly lit interrogation room, where Wendell Shane was sitting at the table alone, still in handcuffs, wearing a thick red cotton sweater, blue jeans, and sneakers. An officer was inside, guarding him. Kayla motioned him out as he and Randall sat down opposite Shane at the table. "Hello, Wendell. I'm Detective Kayla, and this is Randall Arthur, the man who lives in the house you were caught at. He's also a private investigator. That's why he's here. I want you to tell us why you were outside Mr. Arthur's home this afternoon."

"I'm not talking without my lawyer here with me."

Randall and Kayla looked at each other, both knowing that would be his response to the question.

Randall said, "Look, you were probably looking to break into my home. The cops happened to be driving by. They saw you. They got out and approached you to see what was going on. You freaked out and ran; too bad about that slippery snow that threw you to the ground so the cops could arrest you. And I know why you wanted to break into my house. You were looking for a DVD I have in my possession that someone wants very badly."

Shane looked at both Randall and Kayla. "I'm still not talking without my lawyer. That's my right."

"Yes, Wendell, it is," said Kayla.

"Joe, can I talk to you outside for a moment?" asked Randall.

Kayla stared at Randall for a moment. "Okay." Kayla looked at Shane. "We'll be back momentarily." Randall and Kayla left the room. Wendell Shane could not see outside the window since it was a one-way mirror, meaning cops could look in the room, but suspects and lawyers couldn't look out. After a minute, Randall and Kayla came back inside and sat down.

Randall said, "I've just told Detective Kayla that I'm willing to drop the trespassing charges against you in return for telling us who asked you to break into my house."

Wendell Shane looked at Randall with a bemused look on his face. "You're lying."

"No, he isn't," said Kayla. "He won't press charges if you tell us who asked you to break into the house. You can have immunity from prosecution if you tell us here and now whom you're working for and in a court of law, if necessary. It's either that, or Randall will press trespassing charges, and possibly attempted burglary charges. You can call your lawyer and discuss it with him if you wish. Your decision, young man."

Wendell looked down at his lap. "Can I think it over for a few minutes?"

"Sure," replied Kayla. "We'll go back out and give you two minutes." Randall and Kayla once again got up and left the room.

"You think he'll go for it?" Kayla asked Randall.

"I don't think he's crazy about the idea of going to jail. Hell, all he did was look around for a way in. I think he'll talk."

They waited two minutes, then returned to the room and sat down.

"Have you decided?" asked Kayla. "Like I said, you can call your lawyer and discuss it with him."

Wendell let out a sigh. "Well, that's the thing. You see...it was my dad's lawyer who asked me to do it."

"What?" said Kayla, looking at Randall in mutual astonishment.

"My dad's lawyer was the one who called me and asked me to break into Mr. Arthur's home and look for a DVD that might be in his office. If I found it, I would take it and give it to him."

Randall's mind was running like a hamster wheel, seeing where this was leading. "Wendell, who is your father's lawyer?"

"His name is Paul Holbrook."

Randall thought, *Bingo!*

Kayla thought, *That son of a bitch!*

Wendell could easily see the looks on the two men's faces. "I'm guessing that you know him?"

Randall had never met the man, but Joe Kayla had, last year after the death of Holbrook's son, Jack, in a drug overdose. A death that turned out to be part of the case Randall was working on concerning a new street drug called Burmese

Blue. Paul Holbrook's reaction to his son's death was not grief but embarrassment and shame. The same had gone for Jack's mother. Kayla had read them the riot act over their heartless reaction to their son's death. The Holbrook couple didn't like it, but Kayla didn't care. Now that Holbrook had allegedly ordered a break-in, Kayla was determined to bring the bastard down.

"Okay, Wendell," said Kayla, "tell us the story. How did you get involved in this?"

Wendell looked at Randall. "I want you to swear that you'll keep your word and not press charges if I tell you what happened."

"I'm keeping my promise, Wendell, and you'll have it in writing and signed by me when Detective Kayla can get it ready. I swear to God above," he said, lifting his right hand, "that I won't press charges. Detective Kayla and I just want the man who asked you to do this, not you. You don't know me and have no grudge against me. And vice versa. Just please tell us what happened."

Wendell sighed. "Okay. I knew Paul's son, Jack, from high school. When Jack died last year, my dad and I went to his visitation, and I paid my condolences to the Holbrooks. A couple of months later, my dad got arrested on a prostitution sting at the Marriot here in town. The cops found an ounce of cocaine in his coat pocket. But it wasn't his. The whore had put it there while he was in the bathroom. Anyway, my dad was in jail for not only solicitation but also for possession of cocaine. Cocaine that wasn't his. He needed a lawyer. I suggested Mr. Holbrook. I called him myself and told him what was going on. He accepted the case and was able to get the whore to confess that she had planted the drugs on my dad. He just got convicted on the solicitation, but the drug charges were dropped against him, and she was charged for planting the drugs on him."

"I remember the case," said Kayla. "Your dad's name is Jeffrey Shane, right?"

"Yeah, that's him. Anyway, after the charges were dropped, I thanked Mr. Holbrook for getting my dad off on the drug charges. I told him that if there was anything I could ever do for him, not to hesitate to call me."

"Which he did today," said Randall.

"Yeah."

"But why would you agree to break into someone's house, Wendell? Risking getting caught and ending up here?" asked Kayla.

"At first, I said no. However, he insisted he would take care of things if I got caught. All I was to do was make sure Mr. Arthur wasn't home, then break in and look for this DVD. If I found it, I was to go to his office and give it to him. I owed him for helping my dad. I was scared, but I decided to take the risk. Dumb idea, I guess."

"Yeah, it was," said Randall. "Didn't you think there might be a security system, Wendell? If you could break or lift a window, the alarm would sound?"

"I thought about it but hoped there wasn't. I didn't know you were a private detective and might have the forethought to have one. All Mr. Holbrook told me was the house's location and what to look for. He didn't even tell me your name."

"He's probably waiting for you to call him now, isn't he?" said Kayla.

"Yeah."

"Go ahead and call him. Tell him you got caught. See if he

comes down here. But don't tell him what you just told us about him. Just tell him you were discovered at the house and got arrested. Don't mention Randall's name at all. Tell him you've refused to talk to the cops until he arrives. Deal?"

"Okay."

"Let me get your phone. Hold on a second." Kayla got up and opened the door. He called over an officer and asked him to get Wendell's cell phone, which had been taken, along with his other personal possessions, after his mugshot was taken. Kayla returned and waited until the officer came in a couple of minutes later and handed Kayla the cell phone.

Once the officer left, Kayla got up, took a set of keys from his pocket, and unlocked Wendell's cuffs from his wrists. "Make the call. We're watching to see if you follow the script, okay?"

"Okay." Wendell dialed Holbrook's number. It was several seconds before he got an answer. "Yeah, it's me. I got busted. A couple of cops were driving by and saw me outside the house. I panicked and ran, but I fell while running in the snow, and they caught me. I'm at the police station now. I haven't said anything to the cops yet. I'm waiting till you get here." He listened for a moment. "Okay, thanks. And I'm sorry it didn't work out." He listened to Holbrook's voice on the other end for a few more seconds, then disconnected. "He's on his way here."

Kayla smiled as he cuffed Wendell once again and took back the phone. "Great job, kid. Okay, here's what's going to happen—the officer outside will take you back to your cell for the time being. I will call the DA and get things set up for the agreement with Mr. Arthur not to press charges. When Mr. Holbrook gets here, we will arrest him on suspicion of arranging a robbery. It will take a little time, but I promise to have you out of here as soon as possible. Thank you for telling us the truth, Wendell."

"Yeah. Thank you," said Randall.

"I'm sorry for what I did, Mr. Arthur."

"I know, Wendell. Apology accepted."

Randall and Kayla once again left the interrogation room. Kayla had the officer take Wendell back to his cell and gave him the cell phone to return to its proper place while Wendell was in custody. Once Wendell and the officer were out of earshot, Randall told Kayla, "Listen, Holbrook isn't going to give up Roger Bowles that easily."

"I know. We might have to make a deal with him to get Bowles. Which I hate to do because I really dislike that bastard, Holbrook."

"I know. But I think Bowles is guilty of much more serious things than Holbrook. He's the bigger fish. We need to figure out why he wants that DVD so bad." As he was in the middle of that last sentence, his cell phone chimed in his jacket pocket. He pulled it out and saw that it was Bryan's number.

"Yeah, Bryan, what's up?"

"Are you still at the station?"

"Yeah." Randall told Bryan what Wendell had told them.

"Damn. Listen, I was going to tell you something else about the telegraph before you got the call from the police about your house. And the more I think about it, the more I think it might be the lead we're looking for."

"Okay, go ahead and tell me."

"When I was a kid, my father and I played these games where we would communicate only using Morse code. One of the ways we'd do it was by blinking our eyes in code at one another. He told us the story about this POW in Vietnam. Denton, I think his name was."

"Yeah. Jeremiah Denton."

"Right. His captors made him appear in this propaganda film that they sent to the Americans. In the film, Denton was able to blink out in Morse code the word 'torture.' The military guys here in the States could pick up on that. Anyway, when you watched my father's recording, did you notice how much he was blinking? I just thought it was natural, or just part of being upset, or whatever, but the more I think about it, the more I think maybe—"

"Holy shit, Bryan, that's it!" He looked at Kayla looking at him quizzically. "Listen, does Roger know you and your dad did this?"

"My father played the game with both of us. So, yeah."

"Damn it, he's figured out what's on the DVD. He knows what Joseph was trying to tell you, but Roger still thinks we're trying to figure it out. Which we are. That's why he wants to get his hands on the DVD. Stick close to your family, and don't let them out of your sight. I'm going home to watch the DVD and figure out what your father was trying to tell you. I will call you back later, okay?"

"Okay. You think I'm right, Randy?"

"Yeah, I think you're right. Talk to you later. And thanks for the call."

"Don't mention it. Good luck."

"Thanks." Randall disconnected and told Kayla what Bryan had told him.

Kayla shook his head and chuckled. "This is getting more and more fascinating, indeed."

"Listen, I'm going home and watching the recording

again; now I know what I'm looking for. Do you need me here for Holbrook?"

"No, I can take care of it. You'll have to sign the agreement, but we can take care of that later. It will take some time to get it drawn up, anyway. Get out of here and figure this thing out. Call me when you do."

"Will do." Randall rushed out of the station to return home and figure out Joseph Bowles' mysterious Morse code.

Chapter Fifteen

When Randall arrived home from the police station, he immediately visited his PI office. He first got onto the Internet and printed a chart sheet of Morse code to assist him while he watched the Bowles recording. Then, he took the DVD out of his desk drawer, turned on the DVD player and the television, slipped the disc inside, sat down at his desk with the code sheet, a steno pad, and a pen, and watched the tragic events of that day again.

Initially, Joseph's blinking seemed to be the normal, involuntary sort that all humans do without thinking about it. But as Randall ran the digital recording back and forth, pausing it here and there, he noticed a particular moment when that seemed to change. It was when Joseph said, "Bryan, I need your help." He then began to cry, but his blinking seemed to slow down just enough that Randall thought it might have become a conscious effort. Randall stopped the disc again and returned to the moment the behavior began. He had the steno pad and chart on his desk and pen in hand, and he carefully watched Joseph Bowles' eyes for the message Randall was now certain he was sending to his estranged son. He continued to talk while blinking the message, but Randall was now only concentrating on the eyes.

He got the first letter:

Three dots: S.

Then the second:

One dash: T.

And it continued:

One dot: E.

Two dots, one dash, and one dot: F.

One dot and one dash: A.

One dash and one dot: N.

Three dashes: O.

One dash and two dots: D.

One dot: E.

Two dots, one dash, and one dot: F.

One dot, one dash, one dot: R.

One dot and one dash: A.

One dash and one dot: N.

One dash, one dot, one dash, one dot: C.

Three dashes: O.

Stefano DeFranco.

Oh my God, thought Randall.

Joseph Bowles had just been able to blink out the last "O" before he collapsed onto the floor of Burt Olivetti's office. As if the effort of blinking out this message would drain all the energy from him, which perhaps it did.

Randall stared at the name he'd written vertically on the steno pad from Joseph's code. He was looking at the name of perhaps one of the most notorious mob bosses ever in the northeastern section of the United States and the western section of New York State. DeFranco ruled the mafia underworld in this part of the state from his mansion in Buffalo for nearly thirty years, from the mid-seventies to the beginning of the twenty-first century, spreading terror and havoc to his enemies.

Even death.

His reign of crime and terror had come to a crashing demise, all because of his son Dominick, whom Stefano was grooming to take over the family business once Stefano died or decided to retire. Sadly for Stefano, the federal government got to Dominick and made him turn against his father by telling all he knew of Stefano's business and past illegal actions in return for complete immunity from prosecution and a lifetime of protection in the United States Federal Witness Protection Program. Because of the betrayal of his son, Stefano DeFranco was convicted of numerous offenses—murder, conspiracy to commit murder, loansharking, illegal gambling, obstruction of justice, bribery, and tax evasion—almost every crime listed under the RICO Act. He was now in a federal prison about ninety miles south of Falcon City, the United States Penitentiary at Strykersville, where he would spend the rest of his life.

Randall was still in a mental daze when he heard the doorbell ring downstairs. He rushed down to see who it was. It was Joe Kayla.

"Hey, Joe. Come on in. Follow me upstairs. I have something to show you."

"Okay." As they walked across the kitchen and dining room to the stairs, Kayla said, "I called the DA, and he's going to get all the paperwork ready. All you have to do is come down to the station in the morning and sign the document that says that you don't want to press charges against Wendell Shane."

Once they were in Randall's office, he asked Kayla, "What about Holbrook?"

Kayla smiled. "Oh, he was surprised when he got to the station. The DA wanted to have him arrested on conspiracy to commit burglary. Mr. DA dislikes Holbrook even more than I do. I questioned him, but he denied everything and said the kid was lying. He's spending the night in jail and bitching about the supposed false arrest, potentially suing me and the police department. You know, all that jazz. I'm hoping he will see what he is truly facing and decide to tell us everything he knows about Roger Bowles. Oh, I got Wendell a public defender to help him out. As for Holbrook, he called up another lawyer to help him get out of this. I love it when lawyers end up needing their own lawyers." Kayla motioned his head toward the TV set. "So, have you figured out the video yet?"

Randall picked up the steno pad from his desk and handed it to Kayla without speaking.

Kayla stared at it for a few seconds and then looked back up at Randall. "You're kidding."

"Do you see me laughing?"

Kayla slowly shook his head. "*Fuck!*" He handed the pad back to Randall.

"Yeah, that was pretty much my feeling on the subject, too."

"What in the hell does all this have to do with a mobster who's been in prison for the last decade?"

"I think there's only one way to find out. Do you have any connections at the prison in Strykersville?"

"Yeah, I happen to be friends with the warden."

"You think you can get me in to see DeFranco tomorrow? See what he has to say?"

"Only if I come with you."

"Deal."

Chapter Sixteen

AFTER THREE DAYS OF INTERSTATE TRAVEL, EATING AT fast-food joints off the interstate, and sleeping in motels overnight, Jay Shidler finally reached his destination of Falcon City at 7:44 P.M. So far, the authorities were still in the dark about the true whereabouts of Jay Shidler, thanks to his and Roger's planning, as well as the kidnapping video posted on the Internet. A second video of Jay's supposed beheading at the hands of Islamic terrorists had been posted online earlier this morning, and Jay was to the rest of the world dead and headless. In truth, the actual videos were filmed two months ago in Nigeria. The hooded terrorists who looked to have Jay at their mercy were some of the soldiers from Jay's earlier mission to kill Kamal Jaden, and the victim of the blade was one of the members of Karfin Allah captured in the raid of Bama. His black hands were tied behind his back, and the rest of him was covered in black clothing so as not to give away the fact that the man about to be executed was not a white man. The Nigerian government owed him a favor for taking out Jaden, and when he and Roger were developing their plan, Jay figured out a way to cash in on that favor.

The last motel on this journey was the Days Inn, just inside the city limits. He signed in as "Peter Bowles." It was Roger's idea. Jay would pretend to be a Bowles family member, a cousin who heard about Joseph's death and came to see the family and pay his respects. That was the story Roger would tell the desk clerk when he came to see Jay to go over the final plans.

Once he got situated in his room, Jay took out his cell, triggered the scrambler app, and called Roger. "Hey. I'm in town."

"Good. Any problems?"

"No. Except it's cold as hell. Definitely not Arizona. How did the situation go with the disc?"

Roger sounded angry. "It didn't go. The stupid bastard, who my stupid lawyer got to break into Arthur's house, got himself arrested. A patrol car was on the street and saw him outside the house. He ran, and they arrested him. Then Arthur and a cop friend of his got the kid to confess that my lawyer asked him to do the job in the first place. Now my lawyer—soon to be my fucking ex-lawyer—is in jail. Thankfully, he's staying quiet about my involvement."

"So far. He might end up throwing you under the bus, eventually."

"This has gotten out of hand, Jay." There was anxiety in Roger's voice.

"Does Arthur know what's on the disc?"

"I don't know. And it's driving me crazy not knowing. I don't know if Bryan has realized what might be on there yet. But if he has, I'm sure he's told Arthur."

"What do you want me to do?"

"We go ahead with the plan. I'll come by in the morning at about eight, and we'll go over things. But there is one more thing we need to do."

"Get rid of Arthur before he can cause us any more trouble?"

"Exactly."

Chapter 17
Saturday (I)

KAYLA CAME AT AROUND EIGHT-THIRTY TO PICK UP Randall from his house. He was driving his car, a blue 2014 Dodge Dart, instead of his assigned police vehicle. Before they headed south toward Strykersville and Stefano DeFranco, they stopped by the police station so Randall could sign the document agreeing to drop the charges against Wendell Shane. Wendell was scheduled for a court appearance at eleven with his court-appointed lawyer to finalize everything so he could get out of jail. As for Paul Holbrook, his situation was stickier. Kayla had called the DA last night and told him of the possible involvement of Stefano DeFranco in the case, and the DA said that would hopefully sway the judge to not allow Holbrook out on bail yet.

Randall called Bryan last night and told him what he had discovered from the DVD. Bryan was as shocked as Randall and Kayla had been. He didn't know what DeFranco might have to do with all this. He had never heard his father mention Stefano DeFranco's name. Randall told Bryan to keep close to his family and that he would call him back later, filling him in on what DeFranco had told them.

Kayla drove the trip to the prison. They were listening to a classic rock station on the radio while talking about what might be ahead. The sky was as cloudy and dreary as it had been for the last few days, still cold, with occasional spits of snow showers. But the weather forecasters had promised at least the return of blue skies tomorrow. The bad news was that without the cloud cover, the temperatures would get even colder, perhaps below zero, and that did not even add in the wind chill factor.

"Do you think he'll talk to us?" asked Randall as they traveled southward.

"I sure as hell hope so," replied Kayla. "Think about it, Randy. He's in prison for the rest of his life. He pleaded guilty to everything the government had on him from his son's testimony. The kid gave them everything they needed to nail the old man forever. Despite his lawyers' urgings, Stefano didn't even put up a fight in court. Maybe he was too distraught over his son's betrayal. Maybe he was smart enough to know he didn't have a chance in hell of getting off on the charges. Hopefully, he'll think he has nothing else to hide that will hurt him."

"Why do you think Dominick did that to his father?"

"Good question. Maybe the kid, who was eventually to take over the family business, came down with a major case of the morals. Or, more likely, the government put the fear of God into him."

Randall sighed as he looked out the window, the landscape of western New York State speeding by. The voice of the late, great George Harrison was coming out of the stereo car speakers as he sang about his sweet lord, a lord perhaps he was already with. "I have the feeling this story is going to get very weird before it is all over."

Kayla looked over at Randall. "Well, since you're involved, it probably will."

"Haha."

They continued southward.

They arrived at the prison around eleven-thirty. It was the only maximum-security United States penitentiary in New York State. The façade was stone with two front and back guard towers and fifteen-foot-high reinforced wire fencing. It didn't exactly have the drab look of Alcatraz, but it was still a place no one wanted to end up residing, especially for the remainder of their life. Construction of the prison began in the late 1990s, opening just around the time when the 20th century was transforming into the 21st, and was already a relatively new facility when Stefano DeFranco had moved in for his life sentence a few years later.

Randall and Kayla showed their IDs to the guard at the entrance shack, explaining that the warden was expecting them. After a quick call to confirm this, the guard gave them laminated passes and let them through to the parking lot. Once they were actually inside the prison building, they had to pass through two more guards, handing their firearms to the first guard. Then, they went up one floor in an elevator, escorted by a guard, to the warden's office.

When they entered the office, Lisa Henderson stood up and walked around her desk. She was a lovely, brunette-haired lady in her early fifties, a veteran of both the state and federal penal systems. "Joe, it's so good to see you again," she said, shaking his hand.

"Good to see you again, Lisa. This is Randall Arthur."

"Hello, Mr. Arthur," she said, shaking his hand as well. "Pleasure to meet you."

"You, as well. Thank you for allowing us to come this morning."

"Joe explained the situation over the phone last night, and hopefully, Mr. DeFranco will cooperate with you in your investigation."

"We hope so, too," said Kayla. "If I may ask, what kind of prisoner has he been since he got here?"

"He keeps to himself a great deal. Very polite to the guards and other prisoners whom he occasionally interacts with. The only visitor he gets is his lawyer. Reads a lot. I think that's how he spends most of his time these days." She paused for a moment. "This isn't public knowledge, and I ask that you keep this between us, but a few months ago, Mr. DeFranco was diagnosed with pancreatic cancer. So, when you see him, you will notice his gaunt appearance. The doctors say he only has a few months left to live. He has refused any treatment for the disease. I think he's accepted his fate and just wants to finish things. Eventually, as his condition worsens, he will be transferred to another federal facility better able to take care of him in his last days medically."

Randall and Kayla looked at each other. "Does he know we want to talk to him?" asked Randall.

"I informed him this morning. He seemed surprised. I didn't tell him what the purpose of the visit was about, as you asked, Joe. But he is very curious why you wish to talk to him."

"Where are we meeting him?" asked Kayla.

"There's a room on the first floor where the occasional TV or newspaper interview takes place. Just a room with a table and chairs. A guard is always present, though I don't expect any issues, especially with DeFranco's condition. The guard that brought you up here will accompany you to the room. I will call down and let another guard know that you are here and bring Mr. DeFranco to the room."

"Thank you," Randall and Kayla said almost in unison.

"Good luck. I hope you find the answers to your questions."

"So do we," said Randall.

They shook hands again, and Randall and Kayla followed the guard to their interview with a dying Stefano DeFranco.

Randall and Kayla followed the guard through two electric sliding doors, doors that would only slide with a swipe of the guard's laminated badge, and then down a long hallway to a room on the right, also accessible only via a badge swipe.

The guard remained in the hallway as Randall and Kayla entered the room, though he could see within the room through the eye-level glass door pane. The room was twenty feet by twenty feet, decorated only by an oak table and three matching chairs, two for the visitors and one for the man who had called this place home for over fifteen years. Randall and Kayla sat down at the table and waited.

While they were waiting, Randall said, "You remember that mini-series back in the seventies called *Jesus of Nazareth*? The one with Robert Powell as Jesus?"

"I've seen it in reruns."

"Have you ever noticed that Powell never blinks when he's on camera? He did that on purpose to give Jesus an otherworldly aura."

"Yeah, I've noticed that. Must be hard to do that, though. I don't think I could do it. Blinking is one of those things you just do without thinking about it."

"Exactly. And in Joseph Bowles' case, we have someone who was consciously blinking to get a message across. I was thinking about that, and that miniseries came to mind."

Three minutes after they had sat down, they heard the door behind them slide open again. Entering were Stefano DeFranco and his guard. DeFranco was dressed in his orange prison jumpsuit, his wrinkled, spotted hands cuffed at the waist. Randall had never seen DeFranco in person before this moment, had only seen him on television, and back in the day, he looked larger than life; a thick, intimidating man, a few pounds overweight, but imposing, nonetheless. Not anymore. The cancer was perceptibly taking its toll on DeFranco's body, inside and out. He looked at least twenty to thirty pounds lighter. The jumpsuit looked a size or two too big for him. His once full face was now gaunt, and his cheekbones were more pronounced. The hue of his skin was no longer that of the proud man of Italian descent but of a man whose life was slowly bleeding away. His once thick mane of hair had receded. He was not bald because he had refused chemotherapy, but perhaps because of his advancing age. The scalp was more visible where the remaining strands of his hair had yet to surrender to their fate.

The guard brought DeFranco to the chair opposite Randall and Kayla. "I will be on the other side of the room just in case there's a problem. The other guard is outside the door, just in case."

DeFranco looked up at the guard from his seat and smiled. "I don't think there will be a problem with these fine gentlemen who have come to visit me today. I don't get that many visitors these days, so why should I be rude to those who bother coming here? Besides, Brandon, I'm in no condition to put up a fight of any kind these days. My fighting days are over. But I know you must play by the rules."

"Yes, sir. Thank you, Mr. DeFranco." Brandon looked at Randall and Kayla. "Gentlemen." He then walked to the back of the room.

DeFranco looked back and forth at Randall and Kayla. "Detective Kayla, I remember you from my days of freedom. I tried to know as many members of law enforcement in the western New York State area as possible, as I'm sure you understand. It's been a while, sir."

"It has. Lot has changed since then, hasn't it?"

DeFranco grinned. "Obviously. Some of us have done better than others. Are you going to introduce me to your friend here, Detective?"

Before Kayla could answer, Randall said, "My name is Randall Arthur. I'm a private investigator in Falcon City. I'm here, along with Detective Kayla, on behalf of a client of mine. Your name came up in my investigation, and we have a few questions."

DeFranco studied Randall for a moment. "Wait a minute...you wouldn't happen to be Randall Arthur, the historian and college professor, would you?"

"I would, indeed. Why do you ask?"

DeFranco laughed. "Because I've read one of your books!

The one about the prisoners of war in Burma during World War II. It was damn good, I must say."

Randall was somewhat taken aback, having his literary talents praised by a convicted crime lord. "Thank you. I assume you got the book from the prison library. The warden told us that you read a lot in here."

"Yeah. Don't have the time for much else. Plus, I was so busy with the business back in the day that I didn't have the time to read as much as I would have liked. Funny how that worked out, huh? I gained the freedom to read more but lost most other freedoms. You self-publish your books on Amazon, correct?"

"Yes."

DeFranco shook his head. "Seriously, Mr. Arthur, you gotta get yourself a contract with a New York City publishing house. You're that good. Just my opinion, but I've read every great historian, from Herodotus, Gibbon, Tuchman, and McCullough. I honestly think you're in their league."

"Thank you. Forgive me, but I doubt I'll be asking you for a back cover book review. No offense."

DeFranco laughed. "None taken. You said you're a PI, as well. Part-time, I presume?"

"You assume correctly. I was in the DEA briefly after leaving college, working undercover in Asia before leaving and returning home. So, I do have law-enforcement experience, as well."

"My, a real renaissance man! I'm even more impressed."

"The warden told us about your medical issues," said Kayla, waiting to get off the subject of Randall's renaissance habits.

"If you mean by 'medical issues' that I have cancer eating

away at my pancreas like Pac-Man, probably spreading to other places as well, yes. You can tell by how I look now that I don't have much time left on this Earth."

"I'm sorry, Mr. DeFranco."

DeFranco smiled. "Are you really, Detective—considering the things I've done?"

"I don't get a thrill from people dying of cancer, even people like yourself, who have caused so much suffering for others."

"Perhaps it's a punishment from God if he exists. Perhaps it's karma."

Kayla nodded slowly. "Perhaps. I'm still sorry."

"Well, I thank you. So, why are you two here to visit a dying man today?"

Randall said, "What do you know about Joseph Bowles?"

DeFranco stared wordlessly at Randall for several moments. Then he said, "More than I ever wanted to, Mr. Arthur. I know that he recently died, and if there's a Hell, I hope with all my heart he's there, burning and screaming non-stop for eternity. I hope that if my God thinks I deserve an eternity in Hell, he'll put me as far away from Joseph Bowles as possible within that realm."

"In other words," said Kayla dryly, "you didn't like him very much."

"Detective, what I felt for Joseph Bowles—what I still feel for him, even after his death—is pure, undiluted hatred." DeFranco looked at Randall. "What does this case of yours have to do with that son of a bitch?"

"I was hired by the son of a bitch's estranged son, Bryan. Before Joseph suffered his stroke that would eventually kill him, he went into a lawyer's office and recorded a message for

Bryan. He told him that his brother Roger was about to do something that would destroy their family. As Joseph spoke on the recording, we noticed he was blinking a lot. We eventually figured out that it was Morse code, a game that Joseph had played with his sons when they were kids. What he was blinking out was your name. My question to you is, why would he do that?"

DeFranco was silent, looking at Randall and Kayla, down at the table, then back at Brandon, the guard at the rear of the interview room. "Brandon, could you please come here for a moment?"

Brandon briefly hesitated, then came toward the table. "Yes, Mr. DeFranco?"

"Is there a way you could join your fellow guard in the hallway, still keeping watch on us? What I'm about to tell Mr. Arthur and Detective Kayla I only want them to hear." DeFranco looked back at Randall and Kayla. "Would you two be all right with that?"

"Yes," said Kayla, looking up at Brandon. "We need answers to questions that possibly might save lives. We'll be okay." Randall only nodded his affirmation at Brandon.

After a few seconds' thought, Brandon said, "All right. We'll be just outside."

"Thank you, Brandon," said DeFranco.

Once Brandon was gone, DeFranco sighed. "Gentlemen, I have pleaded guilty in a federal court of law to everything the United States government accused me of. However, I haven't pleaded guilty to everything I've done. There are some things even the supposedly almighty federal government didn't know about." DeFranco paused, a look of anger crossing his skeletal face. "Things my traitorous son didn't even know about. Now, considering I'm close to knocking on death's door, I think it's time to come clean of everything. Not that what I tell you will increase my sentence for one minute. But just to warn you, it's a long and complicated story. And it's a doozy."

CHAPTER 18

Chapter Eighteen

1982

IN APRIL 1982, JOSEPH BOWLES, EDITOR AND PUBLISHER of the *Falcon City Expression*, had a major problem on his hands, and it was mostly due, he believed, to a mobster living in Buffalo, New York. The problem was that the union controlling the truck drivers who delivered the newspapers to the vending machines and the stores that sold them had gone on strike against Bowles and his newspaper. According to the union's leader, a man named Joe Rizzilli, the major issue was that the drivers felt underappreciated and underpaid for the work they did, especially in the Great Lakes winters that plagued Falcon City, driving up and down the icy and snowy streets in godforsaken below-freezing temperatures just to get copies of a small city newspaper to its sellers. They presently were working without a health insurance plan. Their vacation time was nearly non-existent—only one week per year, paid. Two weeks ago, they had gotten fed up and voted overwhelmingly to strike until they got what they wanted—a health plan, at least two weeks of paid vacation time, and a fair pay raise.

However, Joseph Bowles knew this was not the core

reason for the strike. Through investigative work by two of his reporters, Bowles knew that Joe Rizzilli worked for the Buffalo mobster Stefano DeFranco, that DeFranco was controlling the union behind the scenes, and that he was skimming union profits for himself. Bowles' reporters, Eric Owens and Mark Paulsen, had been secretly probing the DeFranco operation for the last year or so. They were investigating DeFranco in nearly the same way that Woodward and Bernstein had the Nixon administration during Watergate a decade earlier, eventually ending a presidency in disgrace. Bowles and his boys hoped to do something similar to Stefano DeFranco. They wanted to obtain enough dirt on DeFranco, which could be corroborated in a court of law without a shadow of a doubt, which would end his criminal empire and send Stefano and his minions away for the rest of their lives. Bowles dreamed of being hailed as the hero of western New York, whose newspaper had done its civic duty and righted a wrong, eating away like a cancer in this part of the state.

Regrettably, the men Owens and Paulsen interviewed spilled the beans to DeFranco. Knowing that he might stop Bowles' probing if he could hurt him with a newspaper-delivery drivers' strike, DeFranco went to his man Rizzilli and ordered him to rile up his union membership and drive them toward calling a strike.

It took just two weeks.

Now, Bowles was losing money on papers not being delivered and not being purchased. He knew DeFranco was behind the strike and would not surrender to him in giving what the union was asking for. Bowles thought if he did that, he would be under DeFranco's thumb forever, that DeFranco would continue his reign of fear that he held like a Sword of

Damocles over western New York State. He had to find a way to end the strike while keeping his honor and reputation intact. The *Expression* was Joseph Bowles' life. He breathed, ate, and slept with the newspaper in his soul. He might even confess that it meant more than his own family, though he dreamed of his three-year-old son, Roger, one day taking the reins of the business. And, he had just learned two days ago, amid worry over this strike and its potential ramifications, that he was to be a father again. Tara had informed him after dinner, and though it had brought a momentary burst of elation, it did not last. If he lost the paper, he and his family—present and future—would lose everything. Joseph Bowles had to find proof DeFranco was pulling the strings behind the union. Then that would break the strike, the union, and ultimately DeFranco himself.

His two reporters were working on this now—looking for something or someone that would, without a doubt, tie DeFranco to the union. They were presently in Buffalo, doing their best to stay under DeFranco's radar, but they were still trying to find that one link. They had called Bowles last night, telling him they were working on a lead that might hook them up with one of Rizzilli's men, who hopefully would be convinced to connect Rizzilli with DeFranco. Bowles hoped that if they could do that, this insanity would be behind him and that he could fully enjoy life again, including the coming of a new child.

Joseph did not know that the insanity was only beginning for him.

Chapter Nineteen

It began in the underground parking lot of the *Expression* office before he could even reach his car, a leather-gloved hand from behind covering his mouth with a rag drenched in chloroform. Before he could even comprehend what was happening, unable to fight back, Joseph was unconscious.

When Joseph awoke, he found himself tied around the torso firmly with rope to a very uncomfortable wooden chair in what appeared to be a basement, one light hanging and shining in the middle of the ceiling. A metal table lay in front of the chair, on which lay a small manila envelope. On the opposite side of the table was another wooden chair. Stefano DeFranco was sitting in the chair. He was not looking at Bowles but incredibly, intently reading a thick hardcover book instead. Joseph could see the title—*The Parsifal Mosaic*, the newest release from Robert Ludlum.

DeFranco looked up from the page he was reading and noticed that Bowles had come around. He placed a bookmark where he had last read and put the book down on the table next to the envelope. "Welcome back to the conscious realm, Mr. Bowles," DeFranco said with a slight smile.

Joseph took a moment or two to take in DeFranco and the surroundings. "Where the hell am I?"

"Doesn't matter. All that matters is that you and I are going to have a little talk."

"Did you have to kidnap me and knock me out to have this little talk?"

"Would you have come to me in Buffalo or allowed me to visit you in Falcon City if I had requested?"

"Maybe."

"Well, I couldn't take the chance on a maybe. That's why we're here now."

"Could you at least untie me?"

"I could, but I'm not going to. I do have to admit, I enjoy seeing you all tied up and helpless."

"What do you want to talk about? This fucking strike your fucking union is fucking up my life with?"

"My, such a filthy mouth on you. And what makes you think it's my union?"

"I'm not stupid, DeFranco. I know that you know my paper has been investigating your criminal operation. You thought having the delivery drivers strike against me and disrupt the selling of my newspaper would get me off your back. It won't."

"Really?"

"Yeah, really. Your days are numbered, DeFranco."

DeFranco laughed. "All of our days are numbered, Mr.

Bowles." He paused for a moment. "Some people are down to zero on the count. Two in particular. I believe that they once wrote stories for your newspaper. Mr. Owens and Mr. Paulsen."

Bowles' face went white. "Dear God," he said, his voice shaky. "You killed them?"

"No, not personally by my hand. They drowned inside their car in Lake Erie with a little help from three of my associates. They were getting too close to some truths that don't need to be public knowledge."

The look in Joseph's eyes showed nothing but pure hatred. "You're going to pay dearly for this, you son of a bitch!"

DeFranco laughed again. "Oh, stop with the clichéd threats. You're in no position to carry out anything against me, as I'm about to point out very clearly to you."

"Are you going to kill me, too?"

"No, Mr. Bowles. We're going to make a deal."

"I make no deals with fucking murderers."

"Really?" DeFranco looked down at the manila envelope on the table, then back at Joseph. "Do you remember a little weekend excursion you took to a camping lodge on Lake Ontario, not far from Buffalo, last summer, Mr. Bowles?"

Joseph, already in shock over the news of the murder of his reporters, looked wide-eyed at DeFranco. *Oh, dear God, no. . . .*

"Huh, I can tell by your reaction that you do recall." DeFranco took the manila envelope in hand. "What you probably didn't know was that I have friends who work there. When I gained control of the union, I thought it would be good to keep an eye on you. Who knew what you might do someday that I could use against you? And, by golly, you sure as hell did it!" DeFranco opened the envelope and poured out six pictures. He arranged them in front of Joseph so he could see them distinctly. They were the last things in this world he wanted to see. The pictures revealed a naked Joseph and a naked young man in various stages of sex. The looks on their faces were of two men in ecstasy.

"You know, I have nothing at all against homosexual behavior, but as I found out, this young man you were blowing and buggering was a bit too young. Sixteen, to be precise. Last time I checked, that was a no-no in this state. And every other state, as well. He was an intern at the paper named Robert Thomas. Wanted to learn how to be a journalist. Looks like you taught him a lot more." He paused. "Whatever happened to that young man, Mr. Bowles?"

Joseph was shaking despite being tied to the chair. Tears were running down his face.

"What happened to him?" screamed DeFranco in Joseph's face.

"He fucking killed himself!" Joseph took a few deep breaths. "He took a gun and blew his brains out."

"Why do you think he did that, Mr. Bowles?"

"I don't know."

"You're a fucking liar. He couldn't handle the thought of himself giving into temptation and allowing an adult male to seduce him. But that's what you did, isn't it? You liked the way he looked. He was indeed a handsome young man. Maybe you wanted something a little different in your sex life, something your wife couldn't give you. He certainly had something she didn't."

Joseph was crying harder now, humiliated like he had never been before. All he could do was nod.

"Mmm. Be a shame if your lovely wife were to find out, wouldn't it?"

"You wouldn't dare."

DeFranco laughed. "Of course, I would, Mr. Bowles. And here's what else I'm going to dare to do. Let me tell you about the deal we're going to make, and then you can think about changing your position. However, with the possibility of these pictures greeting a mass audience, I'm sure what your answer will be.

"First of all, we end this strike. You give the drivers everything they want. The health insurance plan, paid by you, the two-week paid vacation, and a reasonable pay raise. The drivers will return to work a happy bunch, and you'll have your papers delivered to all the places they're supposed to be delivered, on time, as usual. Just like before."

"What else?" Joseph asked weakly.

DeFranco sighed. "Your two intrepid reporters must have notes hidden away somewhere, in a supposed safe place, which detail my operation, especially where the union is concerned. My men couldn't find anything or get them to confess their whereabouts. I think you know where that information is located. I want you to give me that information."

"Fuck you, you crooked Italian bastard."

DeFranco's face grew red. He got up, walked around the table, and slugged Joseph in his tear-stained face with his right fist that bore a ring on the proper finger, knocking him over, still tied to the chair. "That was *not* the correct answer!"

Bowles was bleeding under his left eye where DeFranco's ring had connected. DeFranco lifted Bowles back up into a sitting position. "Now, let's try this again. The third thing you'll do is the thing I had to give a lot of thought to. I wondered how I could truly punish the man who dared to ruin my way of life. Kill him? Just release the pictures of you fucking that young boy? No, killing you wouldn't work. And releasing the pictures isn't enough for me. It would have to be something that you would have to live with for the rest of your life, something that would cause you great pain every day for the rest of your life. Then, it came to me. What's the worst thing that can happen to someone besides death? What could I do to you that would make you regret the day you ever heard my name or tried to take me down? What lesson would be hard enough to make you realize your foolish error? Let me ask you a question, Mr. Bowles—your newspaper has been in your family since the turn of the century, correct? First your grandfather, then your father, then you?"

"Yes."

"How do you feel about your paper? How much do you love it?"

"You're not taking my paper."

"You didn't answer my question. How much do you love it?"

Bowles looked at DeFranco, still with utter vile. "I inherited it from my father. He made me promise to keep it in the family for all time, never to sell it to any outsider. The *Expression* was always to be a Bowles-owned entity. When I die or decide to retire, my son, Roger, will inherit it."

"What about your other child?"

Bowles' eyes widened, horrified again. "How in God's name do you know about that?"

"You mean how do I know that your lovely wife is

expecting and that you just found out the other day? Let's just say I have my sources, like a good newspaperman like yourself would. But let me tell you what I've decided. I'm not going to hurt any of your family members physically. Not now, that is. But the deal we're going to make is that upon your death, I, or whoever is running my family operation at the time, will kill not only your youngest child, whether that be the child your wife is presently carrying or some other child in the future but any family they might form—wife, children of their own. And if you die before they get to that stage, then they'll have a short childhood. If you tell anyone about this meeting today, or the real cause of death of your reporters, what they found, or that I have any connection to the drivers' union whatsoever, then that child will die. Even if I have to kill your wife as well while the child is in her womb, even if I have to cut her open and rip the fetus out myself. Either you agree to this, or I will perform a hostile takeover of all stock in your newspaper. I will buy out every stockholder, and that paper will become a DeFranco operation instead of a Bowles operation. And I'll still release those pictures to the public to show the stockholders, your family, and the rest of the world how unworthy you are to pretend to be a community pillar. You either lose your precious newspaper and have the world know you like to bugger teenage boys, or you simply lose a child. Think of it this way—you won't even have to live to see that child die. Only upon your death will the sentence be carried out. However, you will have to see that child grow up, knowing its fate, and not being able to do a damn thing about it unless you want to lose your paper, break that precious promise to your daddy, and have yourself revealed as a pedophile."

Though Joseph loathed accepting the deal, he knew in his

heart that DeFranco was holding all the good cards, and all he had was a busted flush. So, instead of cursing DeFranco again, at least verbally, he said, "Do I have your word that you will not try to buy out my newspaper, and not kill my youngest until after my death, and not release those damn pictures, if I give you all you want? Do I have your word of honor on that?"

"You have my word of honor, Mr. Bowles."

"No written contract, no handshake. Just your word?"

"Mr. Bowles, in the world I've chosen to live within, word of honor means everything. You might even say it's one of the few honorable things in a mostly dishonorable world."

Joseph Bowles, a man with power and prestige in the city of Falcon City, New York, now weakened, tied to a chair in the basement of a place unknown to him, tears beginning once again to run down his bleeding face. A man who, even though he would not lose his greatest possession and keep his darkest secret dark, felt utterly defeated. "I accept your deal."

DeFranco smiled. "Wonderful!" Then he got up and left the basement. Joseph Bowles would not see him in person again for another twenty-one years. Still, DeFranco's presence would be with him always, especially when he looked at the son to be born in early January 1983, a son sentenced to have a short life, not to live much longer past the death of his father. A son with whom, along with his older brother, he would play games using Morse code. A son who decided in his teenage years to become an artist rather than become part of the newspaper business, not that it would matter much in the end. However, that decision made it somewhat—but not much—easier to cast away that son for his decision to deny the family birthright, easier to disown that doomed son.

Not long after DeFranco left, another man, a rather large

man wearing leather gloves, came into the basement. Bowles guessed he was probably one of DeFranco's henchmen. He took out a handkerchief laced with chloroform and covered Joseph's face, once again sending him into the world of the unconscious.

That darkness would seem a sweet relief after what Joseph had experienced in the last few nightmarish minutes.

Chapter Twenty

2002

Dominick DeFranco began having second thoughts about the future his father, Stefano, had planned for him between his freshman and sophomore years of college.

He was majoring in Business Administration at SUNY Buffalo, learning all the skills it would take to lead the DeFranco empire into a new, high-tech age, when the time came and his father either voluntarily handed over the reins or when he died. During the summer of 2002, when Dominick was about ready to return to the university for his sophomore year and was staying with his family during the summer at the DeFranco mansion in Buffalo, they held a discussion over the future of the family business in Stefano's spacious, book-lined study. Stefano was sitting behind his rosewood desk, smoking a cigarette, while Dominick sat before his father in a plush leather chair. He was concerned about the direction of the family business and wanted to voice it to his father.

"Dad, I think it's time to cut down on the aspects of the business that are considered illegal by the authorities. The bookmaking, the prostitution—all of that. Maybe we should think about getting into more legit, yet still profitable, businesses."

"And why would I want to do that?"

Dominick sighed. "Because, honestly, I think you're pressing your luck by still being involved in all the illegal activities. We've had too many close calls over the years, with the feds and the local cops almost finding out about that stuff. Admittedly, you have done a good job in keeping things like that on the down low, but eventually, your luck is going to run out."

"Son, I have so many law enforcement officials under my thumb that I honestly don't worry about that as much as you do. I've been running this operation since before you were born. I know what I'm doing. When you were a child, some nosy reporters from the *Falcon City Expression* newspaper got too close for comfort. They were taken care of, permanently."

Dominick was shocked. "Are you talking about the two reporters found dead back in the eighties here in Buffalo? The two they had to drag out of the lake?"

"Yes."

"You never told me about that."

"I never felt the need to. I've always found that the less you talk about matters like that, the better, even to family."

Dominick sighed again, got up from his chair, and walked to one of the windows. "This is exactly what I am talking about, Dad. You just love to walk the tightrope, tempting fate. Look, I understand your point. We've done rather well over the years. We have all the money we could ever want, all the material possessions we could ever want, and we live better than most people do. The DeFranco name is respected and feared in this part of the country. It's the feared part that worries me, though."

"Fear has been a major reason for our success."

"Look at nearly every organization that has dealt in illegal activities over the years. Look where they are now. They're either in prison for life, or they've been murdered. I don't want either one to happen to you."

"I appreciate your concern, my son, but I have no plans, or desire for that matter, to go 'legit,' as you put it. I've had no indications so far, save for your concerns, that we are in any danger of facing arrest or prosecution. Anyway, right now, the federal government and law enforcement are more concerned about catching Muslim terrorists than they are organized crime bosses here in America. I plan to give you a healthy and prosperous business when the time comes for me to step aside, or after I die."

"Will you at least think about what I've said, Dad?"

Stefano put out his cigarette in the glass ashtray on his desk, got up, walked around the desk, and hugged his only son. Then, after kissing him on both cheeks, he said, "I will think about what you have said. However, I seriously doubt that I will change my mind. I've done things in this fashion for too many years to suddenly change ways."

Disappointed but unsurprised, Dominick said, "All right, Dad. I'm going to bed now. Love you. Goodnight."

"I love you, too, Dominick. Goodnight."

What neither of them knew was that their conversation had been audibly picked up by several miniature listening devices planted in secret and strategic locations within the study. They didn't know that two men were inside an unmarked gray van near the mansion listening and that one of the men turned to the other with a big smile and said, "Bingo."

When they heard Stefano's phone call just a few minutes after Dominick had left the room, their smiles grew wider.

Chapter Twenty-One

The beginning of the end of life, as the young man Dominick DeFranco had known, began with a phone call the day after the conversation with his father. Dominick was eating lunch alone at a McDonald's about a mile from the DeFranco mansion—a Big Mac, large fries, and a large Coke. He had a table beside the window, looking into the parking lot. His cell phone vibrated in his shirt pocket as he was munching on a fry.

He chased the fry down with a sip of Coke, took the phone from his pocket, and answered. "Hello."

"Is this Dominick DeFranco?"

"Yes, it is. How may I help you?"

"That is what we'd like to discuss with you, sir. How you can help us. And how we can help you, as well."

"I have no idea what you're talking about. You had better cut it with the cryptic comments and cut to the point, or I am ending this call."

"We know what your father did to the two Falcon City newspaper reporters in Buffalo twenty years ago. We know you first learned of this last night in a conversation with your father in his study."

It was then that Dominick realized that the moment he had feared, the moment he had warned his father about last night to no avail, had finally come to pass. With the instinct of someone who had grown up in a mob family, he knew that the law enforcement authorities, be it federal or otherwise—but most likely the feds, had somehow obtained access to the DeFranco mansion and infested it with electronic bugs.

Goddamn it!

"Mr. DeFranco, are you still there?"

"What is it you want?"

"Do you see the white van outside your window?"

Dominick glanced outside and saw the van, a 2002 Chevrolet Express Cargo. He'd seen it when he had sat down to eat but thought nothing of it. "Yes."

"Finish your meal, walk out of the restaurant, and get in the van's side door. We'll take you to meet with someone who can help you out of this mess. It's up to you, Dominick. What do you say?"

Dominick thought it over briefly. "All right. I'll be right out. I've suddenly lost my appetite."

"Good choice, Dominick. We'll be waiting." The man on the other end of the line hung up.

Dominick turned off his phone and slipped it back into his pocket. He looked down at what remained of his fast food, got up, left the restaurant, walked over to the van, slid open the side door on the van's right, and climbed inside.

Once inside the van, Dominick saw two men in suits on the back bench seat. One of them blindfolded him. The next thing Dominick heard was one of the men telling the driver up front to drive. Dominick sat blinded between the two men while several minutes and several miles passed. In about what Dominick guessed was fifteen minutes, the van slowed down, made a right turn, drove slowly a little way up a slight incline, and stopped. The two men herded Dominick out of the van, still blindfolded, and guided him to wherever they were. The door opened, and Dominick was led down what he assumed was a hallway into a room on the left. Once the door was opened, one of the men removed the blindfold from Dominick's eyes.

He found himself in a sparsely furnished room, with just a desk and a hard oak chair in front of it. The two men in suits walked around the desk and stood behind the man seated there. He, too, was dressed in a suit but looked slightly older than the other two men, with thick gray hair stylishly barbered.

"I know you," Dominick said to the seated man. "You're Stephen McKenzie, the U.S. Attorney for the Western District of New York."

"Yes." McKenzie looked to his left. "This is FBI Agent Richards." Looking to his right, he said, "And this is FBI Agent Clifford."

"Am I under arrest, sir?"

McKenzie smiled. "No. Not yet, that is. Whether you are arrested depends greatly on the conversation we're about to have. Please, Mr. DeFranco, have a seat."

Dominick did so. "So, what is this about? I can guess that you and your friends here bugged my family's mansion.

That's how you know what my father told me about the reporters, right?"

"Yes. And a federal judge approved the listening devices. We have had your father under surveillance for several months. We are going to bring him to justice, once and for all. Whatever is decided here today will not alter that. But you have the power to decide what your fate is."

Dominick stared at McKenzie for several seconds. Then he chuckled. "Don't tell me—you want me to testify against my father, right?"

"You know a lot about his operation. Perhaps as much as anyone. We know he's grooming you to take it over one day. After all, you're an only child. You're it. But we also know a couple of other facts. First, you want the business to go legitimate. You told your father that last night. He rejected the idea. Secondly, deep down, you'd rather be an enforcer rather than a godfather. You don't want to be behind a desk, running things. You want to be in the trenches, taking people out, using those great martial arts skills you've honed since you were a teenager. You have trophies galore on your case in your room at the mansion. You're a fighter at heart, not a businessman. You'd rather take people out yourself than give the orders for others to do it. However, your father will never let you be an enforcer or an assassin. And it's too late for the business to go legitimate, as you wish. Like I said, we have your father and his illegal operations dead to rights. We have enough evidence now to put him away for a long time. That's without your testimony. But I want everything on him. You can give us that, Dominick."

"And what would I receive in return? A lifetime in hiding under your Witness Protection Program?"

"Normally, that would be the case. But I have another option for you to consider, something a little different—something that I have discussed with my boss, the United States Attorney General. How would you like to use your martial arts skills, plus other new skills that will be taught to you, for a good cause? An excellent cause. Working for your country."

"What? The fucking CIA?"

"No, the United States Army. Special Forces, to be exact. Also known as the Green Berets. The most elite of the elite in the Army are currently in Afghanistan. We have a lot of enemies in that part of the world, enemies who, less than a year ago, killed nearly three thousand people in one day on our soil."

"Yeah, I remember," Dominick said with a hint of sarcasm. "I had several friends in the towers that fucking day."

"We know that. You'll be given complete immunity from prosecution. We'll give you a new identity after you testify against your father in court. A new history. A new future. Everyone will believe you are under federal protection, which, in a sense, you will be. However, you'll also be a soldier in our armed forces, fighting the good fight instead of fighting in the morass of the mafia."

"And what happens if I survive Afghanistan and eventually decide to leave the Army? What then?"

"You'll keep your new identity as a veteran. You'll have to stay away from western New York, away from any place where your father's associates might find you and realize who you are. But you can live any other place in the world as long as you stick to the new identity we give you."

"And what if I say fuck you to this whole crazy idea?"

Family Dynamics

McKenzie looked at Clifford. "Let Dominick hear what we recorded last night."

"Yes, sir." Clifford pulled a small tape recorder from his suit pocket and handed it to McKenzie, who placed it on the table before him.

"After you finished your talk with your father and left the room, he made a phone call. This is what we recorded." He pressed the play button.

"This is Stefano DeFranco."

"Yes, sir. What can I do for you?"

There was an audible sigh from DeFranco. "My son Dominick wants to turn the business legitimate. He knows things that could pressure me into doing such a thing. But that cannot be allowed to happen. Do you understand?"

"Perfectly, sir."

"After you've done it, send me proof of his death, then bury the body somewhere. Let's make it look like a disappearance, Jimmy Hoffa-style."

"I've never let you down before, sir. I will not do so this time."

"I know that."

"I know this is difficult for you, sir."

"No—it isn't. He is my only heir. But his plans will ruin our operation. That I cannot allow to happen, son or not. I will have to make new arrangements for the future of my organization, ones that don't include Dominick."

"Understood, sir. I'll get to work on it right away."

"Thank you. Goodnight."

"Goodnight, sir."

McKenzie hit the stop button on the recorder. "Now we have him on tape planning the murder of his son. The van that brought you here isn't ours. It belongs to the enforcers your father sent to kill you. We got to them before they could get to you, and now they're helping us to convince your father that they indeed carried out their mission and killed you. At least, convince him for the time being. This is your only way out, Dominick."

Dominick sat there, saying nothing, stunned and heartbroken. His father had put a hit out on him. There would be no legitimizing of the family business. Stefano was determined to stick to his old ways, so determined that he was willing to kill his only son and heir to maintain the status quo. Dominick knew now that he didn't have a choice if he wanted to stay alive.

"If I accept this, I know you can't promise my protection in the middle of a war. Hell, it might work out for the best if I was killed. But if I do come out of it alive, what happens afterward? After my soldering days are over and I return to civilian life, I want to know that you'll have my back then."

"We will keep your new identity as secret as possible, along with your location. For now, we'll need to perform some makeup work on your face to make your father believe you were shot in the head. He'll see that and think you're out of the picture, as he wanted. What do you say, Dominick?"

He thought about it for a brief time. It was either this or death at the orders of his father, a father he loved, a father he thought loved him. That was the choice, nothing else. He sighed. "Okay, tell me what the fuck you want to know."

Chapter Twenty-Two

2003

Joseph Bowles was the first person ever to visit Stefano DeFranco in prison, who wasn't his attorney.

"Come to gloat?" asked DeFranco once Bowles had sat down across the table from him in the same room where DeFranco would be telling his story to Randall Arthur and Joe Kayla nearly a decade and a half later.

"Tempting as that is, no. Though I must say that seeing you in prison in that orange outfit is the best sight I've seen in years."

"Then why in the fuck are you here?"

"I'm here to tell you that our deal has been rescinded. The moment you were sentenced in that Buffalo federal courtroom, all your crimes out in the open, that deal you forced me to accept twenty-one years ago became null and void. You have nothing over me anymore except those pictures. However, if you decide to still make them public after all these years, I will just say you had them doctored. I'm sure you know people who can expertly do such a thing. I'll say you had it in for me because of the 1982 strike. And if you claim I agreed to have my youngest son murdered, I will say that is a lie, too. Whom are people going to believe? A highly respected newspaper publisher or a mobster in jail for the rest of his miserable life? Let me ask you—did you have that conversation we had recorded?"

"No. I admitted certain things in that conversation, too. I would have been a fool to record that purposefully. However, I was a fool not to realize that the government had me bugged. Thanks to them and my son, I've lost everything."

"You did this to yourself, DeFranco. You thought you were Teflon, like Gotti. Both of you were cocky as hell and paid the price. Your son was smart enough to see that he had no other option. You talk about me being willing to let my son die? You put a fucking hit out on yours just because he wanted to make the business legitimate. You weren't coerced into that like I was. You made that decision of your own free will."

"He would have destroyed my business by trying to legitimize it."

"He did destroy your business. He and the feds. Looks like you were ultimately screwed either way."

"You've done what you came here to do, Bowles. The deal is off. Now please get the fuck out of here."

"Sure. But before I go, I have one more thing to say to you, DeFranco. I hope you rot and suffer in this prison for all the pain and suffering you've caused. Not only to myself but also to the families of the two good men who worked for me. The men you had murdered twenty-one years ago. All people like you get what they deserve, sooner or later. Now, at least when my time is over, I will have the satisfaction of knowing that my son is safe and that you are no longer in a position to harm him or anyone else ever again. And, by the way, I want the pictures. Hopefully, you have them somewhere safe where the authorities didn't find them during or after your arrest."

"I do. I will have my attorney deliver the sealed envelope to you."

Bowles rose and started to walk away but then stopped, turned around, and displayed the middle finger of his right hand to DeFranco. "Fuck you, you crooked Italian bastard." Joseph could see DeFranco's face redden in anger, remembering the last time Bowles had told him that, eleven years ago. Bowles couldn't help but smile as he walked out of the visiting room, never to look at Stefano DeFranco again. He walked away from his nemesis of the last two decades, feeling that his nightmare was finally over.

How wrong he was.

DeFranco meant to keep his word about delivering the pictures to Joseph. But that all changed when Joseph gave him the finger and cursed him. He thought about it for a moment before contacting his lawyer and asking for the envelope to be delivered. Not to Joseph Bowles, but to his wife, Tara, at the Bowles home one morning when Joseph was at the office. Two days after Joseph visited the prison, a hired deliveryman came to the house and gave Tara the envelope, saying only that it concerned her husband. He quickly left without even worrying about a tip; the lawyer had compensated him enough to satisfy him.

Tara, puzzled by what had just happened, entered the living room, sat in a chair, and opened the envelope that had yet to be opened in twenty-one years. She went through the pictures one by one, her mind trying to grasp what the images showed and the impossibility of it.

She had been through the fight with her demons for many years, a fight she needed pharmaceutical assistance with, a fight she endured every day, some days better than others. Part of that was the belief that her husband, a man she truly loved, did not love her as much. A man who loved his newspaper more—even more than his children. Although he interacted with them like a good father and had been a good husband to her, she could always sense a distance from him. It was as if he would rather be somewhere else, most likely in the bustle and hum of the newspaper office, getting the paper ready each day, making it the best paper he could. However, now there was proof that not only had he cheated on her, though by the look on his face, it appeared to be a much younger Joseph Bowles, but he had done it with someone who appeared to be a teenage boy!

Dear God, why?

This was just another demon she could not fight, would not fight. She knew she would lose. So, tears in her eyes, she put the pictures back in the envelope, went upstairs, and wrote a goodbye note to her family, including Bryan, whom Joseph had so heartlessly ostracized for not wanting to follow in the family's footsteps, which added yet another demon for her to wrangle with.

In her note, she spoke about how she was tired of the fight and then took every pill she had left, four different depression and anxiety medications, a cocktail she knew would be lethal. Lying down in bed with two envelopes in her right hand, she waited to die. Thankfully, she didn't have long to wait.

Joseph found her dead body two hours later. He took the suicide note and the lewd, incriminating pictures he had not seen in so long from her person. In his grief and disgrace, he knew that, despite his utter optimism two days ago, Stefano DeFranco had beaten him again. Only this time, it was from a prison cell.

Chapter 23

Saturday (II)

"So," said Stefano DeFranco, "I'm sure you have many questions." He had just concluded his story to Randall and Joe Kayla.

Randall and Joe shared a look. Then Randall said, "Yeah, we do. First, were you prepared to go through with the deal you initially made with Joseph Bowles?"

"I assure you, Mr. Arthur, that I was. The only reason there is no longer a deal is because I ended up in here, and my power to carry out the deal pretty much evaporated."

"Dear God, do you even have a soul?"

DeFranco smiled at Randall. "We all have souls, Mr. Arthur. Some are just darker than others. Perhaps I was cursed with such a soul. You couldn't be in the business I was in and be a nice guy. I did what I had to do to survive."

"And look how it all worked out for you," said Kayla.

"Most of us who choose this life usually end up on the wrong path. Either murdered or in jail. Not sure which is worse. In my case, the cancer that is eating away inside me can't finish its work soon enough."

"Did you have any contact with Dominick after you were arrested?" asked Kayla.

"No. The last time I ever spoke to him was that night in my study before the feds got to him. I was shown the photo that I discovered later was taken by the feds, showing an apparently dead Dominick. The assassins I'd sent to kill Dominick had turned on me as well. Most people believed he had truly disappeared, perhaps attacked by one of my business enemies. That's what I wanted them to believe. You can guess my shock and anger when I discovered the truth."

"Why do you think Dominick did it?" asked Randall. "I mean, besides him finding out that you were going to have him killed. Were the two of you having issues besides his wanting to make the family business legitimate?"

"No. He was going to be my heir. He was going to take our business to new heights, to places the opportunities of a new century offered. He was a brilliant young man."

"You speak of him in the past tense. As if he were dead."

"He is in the past tense to me, Mr. Arthur. Dominick is dead, as far as I'm concerned. And thanks to the feds, he doesn't even have that name anymore."

"Do you ever wonder where he is now? What new name he has, what sort of life he's living now, whether he has a family of his own?"

DeFranco thought about it. "Sometimes. It's just a natural human curiosity, I guess. But he is no longer a son to me. I can't care too much about his present circumstances."

"Do you still love him?"

DeFranco sighed. "Love, unfortunately, in this case, is not something you can flick on and off like a light switch. So, to answer your question, yes, I guess I will always love him. His blood is my blood. But that makes what he did to me even more unforgivable. And by that, I mean wanting to make the business legitimate. Our business had been thriving the way it was for years. There was no need to change it. Legitimacy would have weakened the business, eventually killing it altogether. He just panicked, and that brought this family down."

"Do you know why Joseph would have sent that message to his son Bryan about his brother Roger?" asked Kayla.

"No. I was in the presence of Joseph Bowles twice in my life—which was two times more than I wish. I have never met either of his sons, so I don't know why this would have anything to do with the deal. That was done and over with years ago."

Randall had a thought that came like a final lock tumbling into place. He tried to keep any reaction from showing on his face. He turned to Kayla, tapping him on the forearm. "Joe, do you have any other questions for Mr. DeFranco?"

Kayla looked at Randall. He had known him long enough to sense that Randall had figured out something and that he didn't want to share it in Stefano DeFranco's presence. "No, I think we've learned all we're going to from Mr. DeFranco." Kayla looked back at DeFranco. "Thank you for speaking with us today."

"I hope you gentlemen find what you're looking for."

"So do we," replied Randall. "Goodbye, sir." Both he and Kayla got up and left DeFranco sitting alone at the table.

Once they had left the room and the guard standing outside had gone back in to take DeFranco back to his cell, just leaving the other guard behind to escort them back out of the prison, Randall said to Kayla, "What if Roger found out about the deal?"

"What?"

"What if Roger somehow found out about his father's deal with DeFranco and decided to take his brother out on his own?"

"You think Roger and Stefano resurrected the deal? He just told us that he's never met Roger or Bryan."

"Do you believe the word of a convicted mafia kingpin on blind faith, Joe?"

"Well—no. But don't you think he was rather honest with us there? He told us things that not even his son knew. If Dominick had known, he would have spilled it to the feds along with everything else."

"Maybe. One thing we know for sure, Roger is definitely up to something. Whether it's in any way connected to this deal is another question. However, it's possible that Roger found out about it, didn't go to Stefano, but decided to go through with killing Bryan on his own."

"But why would Roger want Bryan dead in the first place?"

"That, as they say, is the $64,000 question. Let's get out of this hellhole and try to find the answer."

Randall's phone chimed in his pocket as they walked down the hall. He took it out and saw that the call was from Andrea Rutherford.

Chapter Twenty-Four

"Hey, Randy. I have the research material for the book that we were discussing the other evening. I'm running some errands here in town and thought I'd drop them off at your house," Andrea said.

"I'm not home right now. I'm out of town working on a PI case. But I'm on my way back to Falcon City. How far are you from my house now?"

"Umm, maybe a mile or so."

"Listen, I'll disarm my house alarm from my cell phone app. I know you have a key, so just leave the material on my desk in the downstairs office. Then, when you're finished, call or text me back, and I'll turn the alarm on again."

"Will do. Thanks."

"No problem. And thanks for the material. I appreciate all the work you've done to help me with this book. I'm sure I'll find it beneficial, my dear."

"Anytime. Talk to you later."

"Okay."

Andrea released the call from her phone and headed

toward Randall's house. It was a dreary, cold Saturday in January, but at least it wasn't snowing at present, and the streets had been cleared of the snow that had already fallen. She loved Falcon City, but the winters were getting to her, and she was seriously considering moving to a warmer climate to attain her PhD in a year or two. The labor she had been doing for Randall for his book had increased her desire to pursue her academic career in history. Andrea suspected Randall knew that she would have this reaction, which was why he was so eager to have her as his research assistant. Randall had seen her love for history in the classroom, the same intense love he possessed. Andrea knew it made Randall happy to see the same desire in someone else. That was why he taught and wrote—to spread that passion and interest to others.

Andrea parked her red Honda Civic in Randall's driveway beside his car. She turned off the ignition, took the research material in manila envelopes from the passenger seat, and got out. As she walked across the concrete front porch to the door, she grabbed the house key on her keyring and slipped it into the lock. As promised, Randall had turned off the alarm a long distance from wherever he was.

The miracles of modern technology.

She walked through the living room and down the hallway to Randall's writing office. She placed the envelopes in a neat pile on his desk to the left of his computer. She began to walk out of the office and back toward the living room but halted. Across the hallway was Randall's bedroom. She stepped into the doorway momentarily, staring at the made bed. She and Randall had spent time in that bed, enjoying one another's bodies, moments that would stay with her for the rest of her life, even though she was certain she would meet someone else who would be the true love of her life. Someone she would have children with, someone who loved her enough to share her passion for history and support that passion wherever it led. Randall Arthur would always have a special place in her heart, but her love for him did not reach the level required for long-term commitment, and she knew he felt the same way. But the memories would remain, and they would indeed be sweet.

Andrea decided it was time to stop reminiscing and get out of the house and on to her other errands before heading home for a quiet evening of reading. As she was walking down the carpeted hallway toward the living room, she heard the living room door opening. She immediately thought it was Randall, a smile beginning to cross her face. She was reaching the entrance of the living room. "Hey, Randy, I didn't think you would be—"

Her sentence stopped when she saw the man standing in the doorway across the living room. A man who was not Randall Arthur; a man she had never seen before, sporting a thick winter coat and gloves.

Before she could truly comprehend what was about to happen to her, to fully feel the fear of the utter finality, the stranger quickly brought a gun up with his right arm and fired once, striking Andrea in the forehead, killing her instantly.

Jay Shidler had parked down the street just ahead of an intersection and had walked from the car to the house. When he first arrived, he noticed Arthur's car in the driveway. He was about to exit his vehicle when he saw the girl arrive and park next to Arthur's car. He saw her unlock the door with a key and figured that she must be a friend if she had her key and that Arthur was not presently at the house, even though his car remained there. Did he ride somewhere with someone else?

He had come to kill Arthur, find the DVD if he could, and finish the ultimate mission. Instead, he killed the girl who was unlucky enough to be at the wrong place at the wrong time, and began his search for the DVD.

If Arthur returned home while he was there, that would be okay with him. However, he had a timeframe that he had to adhere to, one that he and Roger had discussed earlier this morning in their meeting at the motel. Jay figured he had only fifteen minutes to do what he had to do at the house.

Jay walked across the living room, stepped over the bloody corpse of Andrea Rutherford, and entered the hallway. He first checked Randall's office. He had no desire to make a mess in his search, and there was no need for time-consuming overkill. He methodically went through all the drawers on Randall's desk. He looked at the desk surface itself, even opening the manila envelopes left by Andrea and looking inside them. He even checked the bookshelves and under the chair and couch. No DVD.

Jay then went into both bedrooms, going through all the dresser drawers, looking under the beds, and even the mattresses.

There was still no DVD.

From what Roger had told him, Jay knew that Randall Arthur was both a PI and a college professor. He figured that the downstairs office was only for Randall's academic affairs. Jay had noticed a door in the office earlier and went back in to see where it led. When he opened it, he saw a stairway and immediately went up to see what was on the second floor.

"Voila!" Jay said out loud. He was now in another office, which he assumed was the PI office.

He went to the desk and quickly noticed the steno pad Randall had used last night to figure out what Joseph Bowles had been blinking in his code. He saw the dots and next to them, the letters descending horizontally that spelled out the name Stefano DeFranco. He stared at the name for a moment, thinking. He also saw an empty DVD jewel case sitting on the desk. Jay put two and two together and reckoned that Arthur had finally figured out something on the DVD that led him to the jailed mob boss. He checked the DVD player and saw that the disc was still inside the machine. He put it back in, turned on the television with the remote on the DVD machine, and began watching it. He saw Joseph Bowles sitting in a chair, talking to his estranged son. Jay had been trained to notice even the slightest of his surroundings, and of people, and he could not help to notice that Joseph was blinking a lot. Damn. He's blinking out Morse code, thought Jay.

He realized that time was of the essence and took out the DVD, popped it back in its case, and slipped it into his pocket. He knew that Arthur probably had made a copy, even though Roger had told Jay that Randall had said there was only one copy, but it wouldn't matter. Jay would do what Roger had hired him to do. He debated whether he should wait for Arthur to get home and kill him or progress to the mission's final phase. While doing this, he walked over to the door he had first seen on his way up the stairs and opened it.

When he saw what was within, he said, again out loud, "Son of a bitch."

It was a *dojo*, the room where Randall Arthur practiced martial arts, a type of room Jay Shidler had used many times.

It contained a large punching bag hanging from the ceiling in the middle of the room, a mat encompassing nearly the whole room, and martial arts-related weapons lying near the walls. He saw Randall Arthur's trophy case that housed all the trophies he had won over the years.

He realized this man shared something with him—a love for martial arts, possibly a love for violent situations. A kindred spirit, of sorts. Jay wondered how a fight between them would play out. Would Arthur's skills be on par with his own? He didn't think so. And as much as he wanted to take Randall Arthur out of the equation as it was presently instructed, he had another part of the equation to solve, the mission that Roger Bowles had hired him for—to kill Roger's estranged brother and his family.

He went back downstairs and out of the house, leaving behind an unlucky and dead young woman. He walked back down the street on the cold, cloudy January day toward his car to finish his mission and solve the equation that Roger Bowles had written for him.

Chapter Twenty-Five

On the northward highway toward Falcon City, Randall waited for Andrea to either call or text that she was finished in the house. Using his cell phone, he went onto the web and looked up Dominick DeFranco. He saw several pictures of him, all taken before he turned federal evidence against his father. A handsome young man with dark hair and chiseled facial features, a young man who was nearly the spitting image of his dad.

However, the son ended up figuratively spitting on the father. The newspaper articles from the period when Dominick was betraying his father in return for freedom from a prison cell said only that he would be put under "federal protection" after he had given his testimony in court. Nothing specific about the United States Witness Protection Program (WITSEC). Although, all who read the articles assumed that was where Dominick was headed.

"I wonder whatever happened to Dominick?" asked Randall.

"You don't think he has anything to do with what's happening now, do you?

"I seriously doubt it. He probably doesn't want anything to do with his family. But, just to satisfy our curiosity, is there a way we could find out? Is there someone in WITSEC who would give us information on his whereabouts if we explained the situation to them?"

"I doubt it, but it wouldn't hurt to find out. Stephen McKenzie, the guy who put Stefano DeFranco behind bars, retired years ago. He may be our best bet. I still think he lives in the Buffalo area, probably the suburbs."

Fifteen minutes after Andrea's initial call, Randall looked at his cell phone and said to Kayla, "She should have contacted me by now. I'm going to call her." He punched her speed dial and let it ring and ring until it went to voicemail. "Andrea, call back or text me to let me know you're okay, please. I'm getting worried." He hung up. "This is not like her, Joe. Something's wrong."

Kayla continued to stare at the road ahead as he drove. "I'm sure there must be a good reason."

Randall looked over at Kayla. "Joe, I'm getting a bad feeling about this."

Kayla thought for a moment. "Let me call one of my officers and have them drive by and check things out."

"Please do."

Since Kayla was driving his private car, he didn't have a police radio inside. He did, however, have his phone. He pulled off the side of the road, keeping the engine running, and made a call to one of Falcon City Police Department's finest, Jimmy Barker."

"Hey, Jimmy. Joe Kayla here. Are you busy now?"

"Just doing my normal patrol on the east side. What do you need?"

"I need you to drive by Randall Arthur's house and ensure things are okay there. There was an attempted break-in there yesterday, and Randall and I believe there might be some trouble there now. A young lady named Andrea Rutherford dropped by to drop off some papers for Mr. Arthur. She was supposed to contact him so he could reactivate his house alarm from his cell phone app, but she hasn't called back yet. Can you check things out to see if we should be worried?"

"Sure thing, Joe. I'm just a few minutes from his house right now. I'll get over there and see what's going on. I'll call you back soon."

"Thanks, Jimmy. Mr. Arthur and I appreciate it."

"No problem. Talk to you soon."

"Be careful. Stay alert."

"Will do."

Kayla disconnected the call on his end, checked the traffic, and pulled back out onto the highway. "We'll know soon if everything's okay."

"It's not like her to not call or text back. Something's wrong."

"Let's not freak out until we know we have a concrete reason to freak out."

"Yeah. Guess you're right." Joe could tell by Randall's tone that he wasn't convinced.

"While we're waiting on Barker to get back to us, let's talk about what DeFranco told us back at the prison. You think Roger found out about the deal?"

"I can't think of any other explanation. Let's look at what's happened so far in this case. Joseph Bowles dies. But before he dies, he discovers that his son, Roger, is about to do something to destroy the family. Joseph is so desperate to stop him that he goes to an attorney, not his own, and records a DVD for his estranged son. However, before he can tell him what Roger is doing, he suffers a stroke and dies soon after that. By the way, I've been thinking that maybe he was blinking out Morse code to Bryan because he had the feeling that he might not be able to finish what he was verbally saying on the recording. When you see the recording, he looks terrible. Maybe he knew that something was about to blow inside him. He says that he isn't feeling well. In desperation, he blinked out Stefano's name, hoping that Bryan would catch it. Anyway, to continue, the lawyer gives Bryan the disc, but he can't figure out what his father is trying to tell him, so he hires me to do so. I question Roger, who denies any knowledge or involvement in any plot that would destroy the Bowles family. I told him that I still had the DVD in my house. Then, someone is sent to break into my home. You and I find out from the busted kid that he was hired by Paul Holbrook, the Bowles' attorney, to break into my home and steal the Joseph Bowles DVD. Then Bryan tells me he had noticed that his father was blinking a great deal on the recording and that they had played games using Morse code when Bryan and Roger were kids. I watched the DVD again and figured out that Joseph was blinking out the name Stefano DeFranco. You and I visit DeFranco in prison, and he tells us of this deal he made with Joseph in retaliation for Joseph investigating him via his newspaper, partly in hopes of ending a newspaper drivers' strike, a union controlled by DeFranco. A deal that would sacrifice Bryan Bowles and his family to death whenever Joseph passed away in exchange for not exposing Joseph's illicit liaison with a teenage boy and DeFranco not buying out the newspaper's stockholders, taking the paper away from the Bowles family. But Joseph rescinds that deal when Stefano's son turns on him and gives the feds enough evidence to put him away in prison for the rest of his life. It's the only reason I can think of. Roger somehow found out about the earlier deal and reinstated it."

"But why would Roger want to kill his brother, estranged or not?"

"Maybe Joseph made an eleventh-hour revision to his will, having a change of heart about Bryan, putting him back in the will. Maybe he gave Bryan too much, which made Roger unhappy enough to want to kill Bryan."

"Okay, then, if that's the case, do you think Roger would kill Bryan and his family himself or hire someone?"

"Roger doesn't seem to me the type to want to get his hands dirty. Most rich people aren't. If he could hire a professional to make it look like a random act of violence, so much the better."

"You think that maybe Paul Holbrook might have hired someone for Roger to kill them? He hired Wendell Shane to break into your house."

"I think maybe the police need to talk to both Roger and Paul soon. And I don't think it would hurt if you guys could somehow keep watch on Bryan and his family until we figure this mess out."

"I would have to contact the Boone County Sheriff's Department since Bryan's house is technically outside Falcon City's jurisdiction. I'll pull over again and make a call to them and get a unit in that vicinity."

"You don't like to talk on the cell and drive at the same time, do you?"

"No. One, it's illegal, and two, I've tried it a couple of times and almost ran into the back of another car each time. So, I decided to stop that shit." To demonstrate his current policy on cell phone talking/driving multitasking again, Kayla found another place off the side of the highway to pull over and make his call.

While Kayla did that, Randall looked out the window at the scenery on the side of the road. It was a frozen, barren farm field. Randall couldn't stop thinking about Andrea, that she should have contacted him by now. He knew in his heart that something was seriously wrong, and he was scared.

Kayla was pulling back onto the road when his cell sounded. He looked at the ID and saw it was Barker calling back. He hit the brake and shifted back into park before his tires touched the road. "Yeah, Jimmy?"

"Joe, I'm here at Mr. Arthur's house, and we've got a bad situation. I entered the home. The door was unlocked. When I got inside, I saw the body of the young woman you were telling me about earlier. She's lying in the living room just off the hallway. She's been shot once in the head. I called another unit to get here ASAP, and we will officially make this a crime scene. They should be here any minute. I think you should get here as fast as possible, Joe."

Kayla was stunned and didn't say anything for a moment. "Okay. We're about an hour from Falcon City, but I will get there as soon as possible. Was there anything else out of the ordinary?"

"No. I went through the house, and everything else looked okay."

"Okay, we're on our way."

When Kayla turned off the call, Randall said, "She's dead, isn't she, Joe?"

Kayla looked over at his friend, knowing his next words would break his heart. He hated the duty he'd been presented with. "Yeah, bud. Jimmy found her body in the living room. Shot in the head. I'm so sorry."

Randall knew the news would be bad when he realized it was Barker on the other end, returning Kayla's original call. Instinct was a powerful thing, whether it be good or bad, and Randall found it impossible to shake the knowledge that developed like a rapid, malignant tumor once he realized Andrea was not responding; something terrible had happened to her. All because of a goddamn DVD.

"Let's get the hell back to my house," said Randall in a monotone.

"On our way." Kayla pulled back onto the road and sped off north, breaking numerous speeding limits.

They were stopped about ten minutes into their rushed return to Falcon City by a New York State trooper. Kayla pulled over and showed the trooper his police ID, explaining the situation in Falcon City. After a quick confirmation call to Officer Barker by the trooper, he offered to give them a speeding escort back into Falcon City, which Kayla gladly accepted. Randall said nothing throughout the whole process, still in shock, still in pain, and anger within him steadily growing at whoever had killed his friend. In the end, he would find this person and kill them.

With Randall and Joe behind it, the patrol car finally arrived at the house. Three FCPD vehicles were already double-parked in front of Randall and Andrea's cars in the driveway, and more were legally parked on the side of the street, with flashers still operating. The police crime tape was already wound around the front porch posts. Kayla parked behind one of the patrol cars, and he and Randall immediately exited their car. Two police officers were outside on the porch, just in front of the tape. They knew Kayla and his friend were on their way, and one of them lifted the yellow tape high enough so they could sneak under it.

Randall and Joe walked into the house and promptly saw Andrea Rutherford's body, concealed by a gray blanket. Randall started to walk over to the body, but Kayla put a hand on his shoulder. "Randy, please don't."

"I have to, Joe," Randall said, his voice breaking.

Kayla stepped in front of Randall and put his hands on his shoulders. "Listen, bud, what's under that sheet is not a pretty sight. I know you've probably seen worse, but she was your friend. We have to have our heads clear. First thing we do is go upstairs and see if whoever did this took the DVD. Then we get out to Bryan's house, pronto, and make sure they're okay." Kayla motioned his head back to the CSI agents taking pictures and samples. "Let them do their thing, and let's do ours. Remember Andrea the way she was in life, not as she is now. Don't have the image of what she looks like under that blanket in your head for the rest of your life, okay?"

Randall was shaking, tears flowing down his cheeks. *Why her, goddamn it?!* Despite it all, he took in Joe's words and finally nodded. He took a deep breath and said, "Okay, let's go to my office."

They walked through the living room, dining room, and the small passageway leading to the stairs. Once they entered the office, Randall quickly went to the DVD player, hit the power button, and then the eject button. He had left the disc inside the player after watching it last night. The drawer slid open. Empty, just as he guessed it would be. Did the thief watch the recording before taking it away with him? He saw the steno pad where he had copied the Morse code, and its meaning, still on the desk. The killer had to see that, as well.

Kayla had gone into the *dojo* for a brief look and came back into the office. "Everything looks in place. Is the disc gone?"

"Yes."

"There should already be a sheriff's patrol car at Bryan's house by now. Call him and tell him we're on our way and tell him what's happened here."

Randall took out his cell phone and found Bryan's number on his contact list. He hit the dial icon. It rang several times until it went to voicemail. He repeated the call. Same thing. He tried one more time. Still no reply.

Randall gave up. "No answer. Let's get the hell to Bryan's house."

They ran down the stairs, through the kitchen, and out of the house to Kayla's car. Before getting in, Kayla asked the state trooper, who was still outside, if he could follow them to Bryan's house, and he said yes. Both cars tore out of their parking places. One minute out, driving through the busy streets of Falcon City, Randall's cell sounded. It was Bryan. Before Randall could say anything beyond "Hello," Bryan said, "Randy, we've got some major fucking trouble here!"

Chapter Twenty-Six

As Jay Shidler approached Bryan Bowles' home, driving on the highway, he immediately saw trouble. A patrol car was parked off the road, on the edge near the mailbox. Jay slowly drove past it and waved to the two officers inside, one man behind the wheel and a female in the passenger seat. The man waved back, and Jay continued driving down the road, keeping to the speed limit. He saw the letters BCSD on the patrol car's door. He knew that meant Boone County Sheriff's Department.

This was their jurisdiction, not the Falcon City PD. Maybe Falcon City PD had asked Boone County law enforcement to keep watch on the Bowles' home. Had Randall Arthur discovered the girl's body yet at his home? If so, he knew Jay had to be on his way to the Bowles' home to take care of business. Was Arthur on his way now? Jay hoped so. But first things first.

Jay drove westward past the guarded house for about another mile before seeing a driveway to his right, where he could turn around. He would play the lost driver who needed directions to get where he needed to be.

Soon after turning around and heading back, Jay saw the house and the patrol car again. He pulled over to their opposite side and got out. As he checked the highway for traffic while advancing toward the driver's side door, the male officer foolishly let down the window. Jay said, "Excuse me, officers, I'm lost. Can you help me?"

Bryan Bowles was looking out the foyer window at the Boone County patrol car and its two occupants parked near his mailbox. Both officers had come to the door just after arriving. They explained to Bryan that Randall Arthur's Falcon City PD friend, Joe Kayla, was arranging for protection for Bryan's family until they could get a handle on the situation. Bryan said he understood and thanked them. Moments later, they went back to their car.

Emily Bowles had been sitting on the living room couch watching a Rick Steves travel show on PBS where the host was cheerfully roaming through Tuscany. Distracted, she was looking toward the foyer, ignoring the beauty of that northern region of Italy and Rick's cheerfulness. "Bryan, maybe you should get away from the window," she said in a loud enough voice that he could hear her.

He replied equally toned, "There're cops outside, honey. As long as they're there, I'm fine."

Emily had gotten up to enter the foyer and now stood beside her husband. "Still, it's making me nervous. This whole damn situation is making me nervous. What do you think is going to happen?"

"Hopefully, whoever is after us will be arrested. Or better yet, get arrested before they show up here."

"But what if he sees the cops outside? They're hard to miss."

"Then he'll probably hold off on his plan."

"I think you should call Randall and his policeman friend and ask them to come here. I'm scared, Bryan. The more protection we have, the better I'll feel."

"I'm thinking about it, sweetheart."

Satisfied, at least for the moment, Emily returned to the living room to watch the friendly and outgoing Rick Steves visiting a Tuscan vineyard. A few moments ago, Bryan noticed a car passing the patrol car, heading westward. He thought nothing of it at the time. Seemed normal enough. That was until he saw the same car return from his right and pull over off the road across from the BCSD car. That didn't seem normal. He saw a man in a heavy winter coat get out of the car, hands in his coat pocket, talking to the deputies. He couldn't hear what he was saying to them, but as he drew closer to the patrol car, the man quickly pulled out a gun and shot both deputies in the head. He then began walking up the driveway to the house.

"Fuck!" Bryan yelled. He turned around toward the living room, standing near the foot of the stairs. He told a confused-looking Emily, "We got to get the kids and get to the basement. Someone just shot both of the cops. He's heading this way! Come on!"

Emily said nothing and bolted off the couch to follow Bryan upstairs. They had talked over a plan of action in case danger arrived. Well, it had arrived. Their basement was to be their safe place.

Their panic room.

The door was heavily reinforced with several locks, and Bryan had several weapons stashed down there. Any potential intruder would have to break down the door after much-concerted effort. If he did, Bryan would be ready for him. He would do anything to keep his family safe.

Bryan and Emily ran up the steps, Bryan yelling at the girls as he ran. "Girls! Come on out! We have to get to the basement now!" Bryan went into Becky's room first. She was coloring in her book on her bed when her daddy came in and picked her up. "Come on, baby. There's an emergency. We got to get to the basement." Bryan's cell phone sounded in his pocket, the ringtone being the Looney Tunes theme. How apt. Things were certainly getting to be Looney Tunes here, and not in a good or amusing way. He ignored the phone for the moment, more concerned about his daughter, who began to cry. "What's wrong, Daddy?"

"It's okay, baby. I won't let anything happen to you, your sister, or your mommy. We just have to get to the basement, and it will be okay. Okay?"

Still weeping, she calmed enough to say, "Okay, Daddy."

Bryan carried her out of the room just as Emily came out with Alicia, who was also crying. They all rushed down the stairs. Bryan's phone sounded again, and once again, he ignored it. The front doorbell chimed as they got to the basement door in the living room between the fireplace and dining room.

Bryan thought, *Is this fucker seriously thinking I'm going to open the door for him to kill me and my family?*

Family Dynamics

Bryan opened the basement door and with Emily and Alicia going ahead of him, they slowly took the steps down to the floor with their children in hand. Bryan locked the basement door with the free hand that was not holding Becky. Once he and Becky joined Emily and Alicia on the concrete basement floor, they all heard the front door crash violently inward, immediately setting off the shrieking house alarm and causing the three girls behind him to scream.

Then, after maybe ten seconds, the alarm abruptly went quiet. The intruder had found the alarm box near the laundry room and shot it into silence with his silenced gun, which they could not hear downstairs. The cell phone sounded a third time. This time, he pulled it out and saw it was Randall Arthur. He was the one who had been calling repeatedly. This time, Bryan answered.

Chapter Twenty-Seven

Once they neared the Bowles home, the trooper led the way with his siren shrieking, and both vehicles pulled up on the shoulder of the highway right behind the BCSD car.

There was no one to be seen inside the police car from their cars. Still, once they all got out and approached the deputies' vehicle, they saw the inert bodies of the man and woman in uniform lying in the front seat, blood and brain matter staining the car's interior, along with the uniforms the deputies wore with great pride in life. They knew that whoever did this was inside the house now, according to what Bryan Bowles had breathlessly told Randall over the phone just a few minutes ago. They saw that the front door was closed, and the shades had been drawn shut, preventing them from seeing what was happening inside.

"I'm calling for more backup," said the trooper, Adam Parker, a ten-year veteran of the New York State Police.

"Go ahead," said Kayla. "Randall and I will stay here for

the moment. Try to figure out what's going on. Do you have a bullhorn in your car?"

"Yes."

"Get it. I'll try to contact the intruder. Hopefully, start a productive dialogue that will keep everyone alive."

Parker rushed to his car, the flashers still functioning as a warning to drivers on the highway, and retrieved his bullhorn from the back seat. He gave it to Kayla, then hastened back to his car to get on the radio for help.

As Kayla was preparing to speak through the bullhorn and as Randall stood beside him to his left, just in front of the passenger door of Kayla's vehicle, Randall's cell phone chimed.

Randall looked at the number on the screen. Just a ten-digit number. Caller unknown. He first thought of not answering it, but his instincts told him to slide the icon across the screen to answer.

"Hello."

"Is this Randall Arthur?"

"Yes, it is. Who are you?"

"I am the man who killed the young lady inside your home earlier today, and I am the man who will kill the Bowles family inside this home unless you do what I ask of you."

Randall could feel the anger rising within him again after a brief respite. "How did you get my cell number?"

"In due time. First, my offer. You come into the house alone and unarmed. Your two friends stay outside and try nothing funny. If you don't, the family dies, and you die with them. I want to talk to you."

"Where are they now? Do you have them hostage?"

"In a sense. They managed to lock themselves in the basement before I could get to them. But locks can be picked. Or shot. It's the least of my talents, believe me. I'm hanging up now, but I'll be watching you and your friends. Think about it, Randall. You're their only hope. Sorry if I sounded like Princess Leia from the original *Star Wars* there, but it's true. You are their only hope. Otherwise, a few more people will join Carrie Fisher in the afterlife." Then, as promised, he hung up.

Randall put the phone back into his pocket and looked over at Kayla. He told him about the content of the call.

"You're not going in there, Randy. Too dangerous."

"I don't think we have much of a choice, Joe. He has the whole family trapped in that basement. He will find a way to get in. I'm the only chance of preventing a massacre here. I know what I'm doing."

"Do you?"

"What is that supposed to mean?"

"Listen, normally I would believe you, but you just saw your friend lying dead in your living room because of that man inside. You want to kill him for that."

Randall looked off toward the gray sky momentarily, then turned back to Kayla. "Of course I do. But I won't risk Bryan's or his family's life because of my feelings. I might be able to stall this guy long enough so one of you can take him out if I can't do it myself. That is all that matters as long as I can keep him out of that basement. Once he gets in there, Bryan and his family might as well be sitting ducks. And if I don't go in, he will kill them. Bryan hired me to find out who was threatening his family, and I'm going to do my job and protect them."

Kayla looked at Randall, saying nothing. He knew he was beaten. "All right. But for God's sake, be careful. Backup is on the way. We'll be here for you. Let me talk to the trooper before you go in and let him know what's going on."

"All right. Thanks, Joe."

"Just fucking be careful."

Kayla walked over to Parker and explained what was going on. After about a minute, he returned to Randall, brought Parker's bullhorn to his mouth, flicked the switch, and spoke. "Whoever is in the home holding the family hostage, Randall is coming inside. He will be unarmed, as promised."

Randall took out his Beretta Model 92FS and handed it to Kayla. "Wish me luck."

"Be careful, my friend. We're keeping watch."

Randall nodded and slowly began walking toward the house, his boots crunching the frozen snow that still blanketed the yard like a nagging memory. He reached the front door. He could see that some of the wood around the edges had chipped away from the intruder kicking the locked door inward earlier. Randall scraped the snow and ice from the soles of his boots on the porch, twisted the doorknob to see if it was unlocked, discovered that it was, and opened it without knocking.

He walked cautiously through the foyer and into the living room. Both table lamps were turned on. The television fixed to the wall was still on, Rick Steves saying goodbye from Tuscany till next time. He saw a man standing midway between the TV on the right and the couch, the coffee table, and two flanking chairs to the left. The man had a gun aimed at him. "Stop right there," he told Randall.

Randall took a few seconds to register the man's face, trying to recall where he had seen it before. It didn't take him long to make the connection. He had seen his picture on his cell phone not long ago.

"You're Dominick DeFranco, aren't you?"

"Well, I used to be him. The government made me take a new name after the trial. But yeah, I'm that guy."

Randall was still thinking through the shock of the revelation. "Roger gave you my number, didn't he? When I called him the other day to arrange the interview. Roger hired you to kill his brother."

"Very good. Your powers of detection rival the legendary Mr. Sherlock Holmes."

"Why the fuck did you have to kill Andrea?"

"Was that her name? The girl at your house?"

"Yeah, that was her name. Answer my fucking question."

"Wrong place, wrong time. Nothing personal."

"You came there to kill me, didn't you?"

"That, and to get the DVD Roger wants. I have the DVD. But I'm guessing you have a copy somewhere? However, you already know what's on it, from what I could tell by the notepad on your desk."

"Yeah. Joseph was blinking out Morse code to Bryan. It was the name of Stefano DeFranco—your daddy. By the way, I spoke to him earlier today at the prison. He told me about the deal he made with Joseph Bowles and how it was rescinded after you turned on him."

"But you figured out that Roger learned about his father's dirty little secret and decided to resuscitate it. By the way, how is my piece of shit father doing?"

"He's dying. Pancreatic cancer."

Dominick didn't say anything, but Randall could see a frown barely form on his face. "Does that upset you, Dominick?"

"The son of a bitch tried to have me killed."

"He told me he still loves you, despite all that happened between you two, though he will never forgive you for testifying against him."

"Fuck him and his cancerous pancreas."

Randall wasn't too surprised to hear that sentiment. "What do you have against Bryan and his family?"

"Nothing. I don't know them. I'm just doing a job for which I was hired."

"So that's what you became in WITSEC, an assassin for hire?"

"As they say, it's a long story. But it's not important now. What is important is the people down in that basement. I'll show you I'm not a completely heartless bastard, as you might believe I am. I'm going to give you a chance to save them. All you have to do is one thing."

"What's that?"

"When I was inside your home, I saw your *dojo*. Very impressive. I don't know how much you know of my past before my father turned on me, and I subsequently turned on him, but I'm a martial arts expert myself. We both started as teenagers, developing and honing our skills. I would like to test my skills against yours, Randall. Fight me. Here, in this living room. No guns, just hand-to-hand combat. Let's see who is the best between us. A fight to the death, Randall. If you win, I die, and they live. If I win, you die, and so do they."

Randall was surprised to learn of Dominick's martial arts abilities. He never saw it mentioned in any of the materials on the Internet that he had been searching through earlier. But, then again, he hadn't dug as deep as he could. Maybe he should have.

Now, he realized he had been lured into a trap.

Dominick had seen Randall's *dojo* and knew that his ego would not allow him to let go of an opportunity to face him one-on-one, to see who truly the better fighter was, the better man—at least on this day. All this case seemed to be about, at its core, was ego and the spreading waves it created once the rock of ego hit the water's surface.

Joseph's ego. Stefano's ego. Roger's ego. Even to some degree, Paul Holbrook's ego.

And now, at the end of the road, as far as this case was concerned, Dominick's ego. And in some way, Randall's own. Because deep down, this was a fight he would not refuse. However, it wasn't just Randall's ego that determined his course of action. A family in the basement was scared to death, not knowing their fate. Randall had to make that fate crystal clear and positive.

"All right. But we fight without our coats, without our shoes. And you put that gun away. Only then do we do this."

"Of course. Let's begin. No funny stuff, Randall. I'll be watching. First, my gun. Though, please allow me to take care of something first. Remember, don't try anything. We really don't need this TV on." Dominick grabbed the remote from the coffee table and aimed it at the television on the wall, showing promotions for upcoming PBS shows. Dominick found the button and turned off the television. As he kept his eyes on Randall, Dominick placed the remote and his gun on the mantelpiece over the fireplace. Then they removed their bulky coats, gloves, scarves, and shoes, leaving them in sweaters, blue jeans, and socks.

"You know I'm going to kill you," Randall said. "For what you did to Andrea, for what you're planning to do to Bryan and his family."

Dominick smiled. "I wouldn't start the trash talk, Arthur. You don't honestly know how good I am. I've been trained by the best *sensei*, not just in this country but in other countries. Countries that treat the ancient martial art disciplines with the reverence they deserve, much more than the so-called greatest country in the world that we are living in."

"I've studied overseas, too, under *sensei* just as revered as yours. And I know of the reverence you speak about. It's true, and I appreciate it as much, if not more so, than you. So, let's see who really paid attention in class, you son of a bitch."

Dominick smiled. "The *sensei* should have taught you never to let your anger get the best of you. Sounds, by the tone of your voice, like you either forgot that lesson or are choosing to ignore it at your peril. Being a teacher yourself, you really should know better."

Randall knew what Dominick was attempting, so he took a deep breath to calm himself and clear his mind for the coming battle. He managed to smile at his opponent. "Not going to work."

Dominick stared at him for a few seconds, then he said, "God, I bet your dick felt so good inside that tight, young, black pussy. Too bad I had to blow the nigger whore's brains out. Would have loved to fuck her myself. I bet she screamed and shook like hell when she came."

Dominick could see Randall's face redden. He watched as Randall rushed toward him to begin the fight, even before he got the last word of his sentence out. Randall was raising his right fist to punch Dominick. Still, before he could make contact, Dominick met him in the living room's center, blocked Randall's right arm with both of his own up in a vertical position, then quickly bent down and delivered a right elbow into Randall's solar plexus. Randall was caught off guard and, with a pained groan, fell backward onto the carpet.

"Oooh. Looks like I hit a nerve in more ways than one. I just assumed she might have been your nigger fuck toy. Mr. History Professor playing the role of Thomas Jefferson. Guess my instincts were on the money."

"Fuck you," Randall said from the floor, still in pain from Dominick's elbow.

Dominick smiled. "No, Mr. Arthur. You and the Bowles family down in that basement are the ones that are fucked. And not in a pleasant manner, I promise you."

"You would really kill an entire family? Just because it's a fucking job?"

"Mr. Arthur, I've killed families before. I do what I must do. It doesn't bother me. As I've learned in my life, families are overrated. Eventually, they end up hurting you. I'm quite content with living my life and ultimately leaving it without a family. Now, get up so we can get this contest started the right way. This was just a prelude, a brief display of what you will be up against." Dominick flicked his hand upwards. "Come on now. On your feet."

Randall slowly rose to his feet, wincing in pain, eyes on his opponent the entire time. He raised his hands in a fighting stance, his left hand slightly higher than his right, and his fingers bent slightly. Taking a deep breath, he mentally tried to slow his racing heart. His solar plexus was sore where

Dominick's elbow had landed, and he thought a rib might be cracked.

"Let's go," Randall said to Dominick.

Dominick smiled slightly and nodded. He entered his fighting stance and immediately threw his right hand toward Randall's face. Randall blocked the incoming blow with his left forearm, which left his chest open for a left-handed, closed-fisted blow to the same spot on the solar plexus, which Dominick executed rapidly. He followed up with a firm sock-footed right kick to Randall's head, knocking him back onto the floor.

Instead of letting Randall back up, Dominick took advantage of Randall's prone position. He straddled Randall's torso and began raining elbow shots to his head, left and right, each one meant to hurt. Randall was helpless. He was dizzy from the foot shot to the head that had knocked him down, and now it grew worse with the barrage of elbows. Dominick had cut Randall's forehead on either side, and the living room carpet was now stained with the PI's blood.

Out of pure desperation, Randall took advantage of an opening to fly out his right hand, impacting Dominick's chin enough to knock him off Randall. Randall forced himself onto his feet, but Dominick was ready, bending to catch Randall under the right armpit and throwing him into the air, sending him flying, landing square upon the coffee table. It didn't give, and Randall screamed again in pain as he landed on his ribs. He could feel and hear the crack of one of his ribs, perhaps two. He had never felt such intense, blinding pain. He had never faced an opponent like this who got the advantage so early and decisively. He knew he would lose unless he did something drastic or unless Joe and the state trooper risked all and intervened. Dominick had hurt Randall enough to neutralize his fighting abilities, while Randall had been so far overwhelmed by his opponent.

Dominick looked down at Randall, who was lying on the table. "Impressed yet?"

Randall did not answer. His head was hanging upside down over the side of the table near the couch. The force of the landing had caused him to cough, which was excruciatingly painful. He tasted blood in his mouth.

"Cat got your tongue?" Dominick bent down to Randall's right ear. "Had enough yet, nigger fucker?"

"Fuck you." Randall shot out his right fist, landing it square on Dominick's nose. Both men could hear the fracture of the cartilage. Dominick fell backward with a yell, bringing his hands up immediately to his broken nose.

Randall raised himself upright on the table, each breath now an exercise in anguish. "Back up has already been called, DeFranco," he said breathlessly. "More cops will be here any minute now. You don't have a chance of getting out of here. Give it up now. You've lost." Randall got to his feet with a grimace and a deep moan. He felt woozy, nauseous, and nearly ready to pass out.

That moment, Dominick took advantage and delivered a vicious strike to Randall's exposed right shin with his left foot. Dominick was looking down as he struck with blood streaming down his face from the broken nose, and saw Randall's leg buckle, heard and saw the bone break.

As Randall screamed, Dominick grabbed Randall's left hand by all four fingers and bent downwards with all his might, breaking them as well, forcing out another wail from Randall. Then he grabbed Randall by the back of his hair and drove his head into the coffee table, almost like a professional wrestler would slam his opponent's head into the turnbuckle in a match nearly as scripted as a fight in a movie. However, there was nothing simulated about this.

Dominick stepped back as Randall crumpled to the carpet, half-conscious.

He stared down at his defeated victim, moaning and bleeding on the living room carpet. "You just aren't in my league, motherfucker. I had to teach you that the hard way, and it will be the last lesson you ever learn." He then walked into the kitchen and began to open the drawers. It took him three tries until he found what he was looking for. A knife with a black handle, with a five-and-a-half-inch stainless steel blade, made in China, last used by Emily Bowles two days ago to chop potatoes and celery for a crock-pot stew she had cooked for her family.

Dominick was approaching the living room, ready to slit Randall's throat from ear to ear when the basement door flew open, startling Dominick. He looked and saw a man he only knew from a picture that Roger Bowles had shown him weeks ago in Flagstaff, Arizona.

Bryan Bowles.

He had a SIG P227 pistol aimed at Dominick.

Without a word, he pulled the trigger.

The bullet struck Dominick in the right upper chest, just below his shoulder. He looked at Bryan, then looked at the crimson wound, then back at Bryan. He somehow managed to hold on to the knife.

"*Padre, perdonami—*" he whispered.

He moved toward Bryan a couple of steps, knife still in hand, and Bryan shot him again, this time in the throat.

This time, he dropped the knife.

He fell to the floor, dead.

In a living room.

The irony.

Bryan took a deep breath. He yelled down to the basement, "I'm okay! He's dead! Stay down there until I tell you to come up!" He closed the basement door and placed the just-fired SIG on the kitchen counter. His hands were trembling. He rushed over to the severely damaged Randall Arthur on the living room floor.

Bryan kneeled beside him. "Dear God, man. Can you hear me?"

Randall half-opened his eyes. "Bryan—"

"Stay with me, Randy. I'm getting help. Stay with me, buddy."

The front door opened as if hit by a gust of hurricane winds. For the second time that afternoon, the door had been kicked in. Kayla and Parker entered along with two more state troopers, another BCSD deputy, and the sheriff himself, who had arrived on the scene while the fight was going on inside. They rushed into the house with their guns drawn, having heard the gunshots and deciding not to wait any longer.

Bryan held up his hands. "Don't shoot." He motioned his head over to the body of the intruder on the floor. "He's dead, but Randall is hurt badly. We need to get him help now."

Randall was trying to process in his concussed brain what was going on. He could see the body of Dominick DeFranco on the floor across from him and had heard, but not seen, the gunshots that had killed him. He saw Bryan return to his side, telling him to hang on and that help was coming. He saw Joe Kayla kneel beside Bryan, saying, "Dear God."

Despite it all, Randall could not speak in the throes of immense pain from broken bones and God knows what else. He steadily felt consciousness leaving him, but he at least knew that the Bowles family was safe.

He could close his eyes now and hopefully fade into unconsciousness so he would not have to experience this agonizing pain within his body.

Chapter 28

Three Days Later

Steadily, Randall emerged from his void to the high-pitched beeping of a heart monitor, the slight niggling sensation of a breathing tube invading the orifices of his nostrils, the inflexible encumbrances of the plaster casts over his left hand and right leg, a thick bandage over his skull and an IV in his left arm. He could even feel a damn catheter in his penis. The primary sensation he felt was the overwhelming soreness and pain throughout his body, from head to toe. He at once remembered why his body felt this way. *How in the hell can I still be alive?*

He slowly opened his eyes and immediately saw the white tile ceiling of the room he was lying in, covered from his belly to his feet with a white cotton blanket. He figured it had to be the intensive care unit of a hospital, most likely Lakeshore Hospital. That caused him to remember that a few months prior, toward the end of summer, he had witnessed the murder of the hospital's administrator and his lover by the administrator's wife, who had hired Randall to discover if her husband was having an affair. That discovery had led to three deaths—one the suicide of the husband of the woman cheating with the administrator, and the other two the victims of an angry, hurt spouse. That seemed so long ago, even though it had been just five months.

Right now, things are much colder and painful. Though the warmth inside the ICU was welcomed, it couldn't eliminate the pain he was feeling now, both physically and emotionally. He looked to his right and saw Rachel, her back toward him, staring out the window. He could see that it was daylight, probably mid-morning or thereabouts. He wondered if she was looking at Lake Ontario and how long she had been here. He wondered how long he had been here.

"Hey, sis. Turn around and stop ignoring me," Randall said in a raspy voice.

Rachel was startled enough to turn around. She looked exhausted. Her eyes looked red and puffy as if she'd been crying. A big smile crossed her face. "You're finally back." She walked over and sat in a chair beside his bed, kissing him on the forehead.

"How long have I been here?" Randall asked Rachel.

"Today is Tuesday. You've been in an induced coma since Saturday because of swelling in your brain. They finally thought your brain had recovered enough to remove the medication inducing the coma. Do you remember what happened?"

"Yeah. All too well. I hurt like hell. Is Bryan and his family all right?"

"Yeah. Shaken up, of course, but they're okay. You saved their lives, Randy."

"Bryan saved mine."

"I know. I'll owe him a big thank you for the rest of my life."

"So will I."

"Let me go to the front desk outside and tell them you're awake so they can check you out. I'll be right back." She remained in her chair, looking down at her brother, beaten up, hooked to monitors, but alive somehow. She started to cry. "Larry and I thought we were going to lose you."

Randall gripped Rachel's hand tightly. "You're not getting rid of me that easily. Now, stop your crying and let them know I'm back to the world of the awake."

"Okay." She sniffed back her tears, wiped her eyes with her fingers, smiled, and leaned back down to give her brother another kiss—this one on the cheek. "Don't you dare go back to sleep on me. I'll be back in a minute."

"Aye, aye." As he watched Rachel leave the room, he remembered what had happened on Saturday. He didn't immediately think about the life-and-death battle with Dominick DeFranco. Instead, he thought about Andrea Rutherford lying dead with her once beautiful head destroyed in his living room. Then he began to cry.

A couple of hours later, after the doctor had checked in on him, Joe Kayla walked into the ICU room.

"Forgive me, Randy, but you look like shit."

"Feel like it, too." Randall's voice was less rough than it had been when he had first emerged from his coma, thanks to a generous sip of water through a straw given by one of the nurses.

Kayla sat down in a chair next to the bed. "So, your sister told me that you've seen the doctor. What's the prognosis?"

"Well, let's see, I have a severe concussion, three broken ribs, a lacerated kidney, a broken hand, a broken leg, and other assorted internal havoc. I'll need surgery for the leg here in a day or two, and I'm sure my exterior has looked much better. Despite all that, he thinks I should be in a private room before long if things keep going well. Maybe a couple of weeks or so before I get out. After that...lots of physical therapy. My teaching is done for the semester, so I'll have to take medical leave until August. And my PI work is done, too. Maybe permanently. Hopefully, I can achieve some writing during my healing time. I did have a research trip planned to Poland this summer. Considering the present circumstances, I might have to delay that for a bit."

"They told me not to stay too long, but I wanted to fill you in on some things from the other day."

"You have a captive audience, Joe. Go right ahead. I'm rather curious about why what happened did happen, considering I'm lying battered and broken in an intensive care unit because of this."

"Okay, first off, Roger Bowles is in custody. And he's talking. With a new lawyer, I might add. Like I hoped, the old one finally decided to throw him under the bus. You were right—Roger did find out about the deal between Joseph and Stefano."

"How?"

"Joseph told him. Joseph was having second thoughts about keeping Bryan out of the family. He saw that Bryan and his family were happy that his comic strip was successful. He realized maybe it was fate that kept Bryan from wanting to be in the newspaper business. He wanted to do something to make up for what he'd done all those years ago. So, he decided to change his will and give Bryan half of everything, including half the stock in the *Expression*. Joseph told Roger that he was doing this. To say the least, though he didn't show it then, Roger wasn't a happy camper."

"Why did he tell Roger about his deal with DeFranco?"

"Confessional, I guess. Joseph wanted everything out in the open. Well, almost everything. Joseph didn't tell Roger about the affair with the boy and the pictures that DeFranco was going to blackmail him with. Joseph just told Roger about the threat to take away the paper and the promise to end the strike back in 1982. He didn't realize that this was a big mistake, as far as telling Roger was concerned. Joseph might have been ready to make peace with Bryan, but Roger wasn't. Though Roger said that when Joseph told him about the change in the will, he acted as if he was good with the idea. However, after their conversation, Roger decided to kill Bryan and his family to reinstate the deal on his own without even telling Stefano that he was doing so."

"How did Joseph find out about Roger restoring the deal?"

"Roger isn't sure. His best guess is that Joseph overheard Roger on the phone planning the murder. Roger also decided to do something else. Not only did he decide to kill Bryan, but he decided to kill his old man, too. Roger has a lot of connections in some shady places. Joseph was taking several medications for high blood pressure. Roger was able to find a guy to supply him with placebos. Then, Roger could secretly replace the real pills with the fake ones. Eventually, Roger hoped, the blood pressure would go high enough to cause a stroke, get him out of the picture, either by death or incompetence due to a stroke or heart attack."

"That was why Joseph had his stroke in Olivetti's office. That, along with the stress of knowing what Roger was doing. Joseph probably had no idea that Roger had replaced his pills."

"I doubt it. But who knows?"

"When Joseph found out what Roger was planning on doing with Bryan, did he confront him?"

"Yeah. That was when Roger told his father that if he told anyone that he was going to kill Bryan and his family, he would reveal to the world that Joseph and Stefano had made their deal and that they had not rescinded it at all."

"Which made Joseph desperate enough to make his recording to Bryan."

"Most likely."

"Did you tell Roger about the pictures of his father and the boy?"

"No. I didn't see the point. Better to let some secrets stay that way."

"What about Dominick? How in the hell did he get involved in this?" Randall would have bad dreams about Dominick DeFranco for the rest of his life.

"A couple of days ago, I got a chance to talk with Stephen McKenzie. My guess was right, by the way. He still lives in the Buffalo area. Orchard Park, to be exact. Not far from the Bills' football stadium. He's had season tickets since the Jim Kelly Super Bowl days in the early nineties. Anyway, he told me Dominick didn't enter the official Witness Protection Program. The government knew about his expert abilities in martial arts, and they knew that he didn't want to take over the DeFranco family business, as Stefano was grooming him to do. And remember, this wasn't long after September 11th. Someone with a talent like Dominick's could be useful in an important arena. Say in Afghanistan, killing those who hated America and loved watching their Islamic brethren crash airliners loaded with jet fuel into three buildings and nearly a fourth. According to McKenzie, Dominick had friends who worked at the World Trade Center who ended up dying that day. The government probably thought the odds were good that Dominick, no matter how good he was, would end up dead anyway in the mountains of Afghanistan. So, they offered him the U.S. Army instead of hiding out in Witness Protection. He took it and did rather well. He became the secret star of the Special Forces under his new name, Jay Shidler."

"Hold on a sec. Jay Shidler? I remember seeing a report on TV the other day about somebody with that same name being kidnapped by Muslims out in Arizona. They killed his wife and sister-in-law and took him away, leaving behind a note. They made a video showing his beheading."

"Wasn't Shidler that got his head chopped off. Roger and Dominick set the whole thing up to make it appear like it was."

"How in the hell did they manage to do that?"

"According to Roger, after Jay Shidler left the Army, he decided to become an assassin for hire. Worked for several years, killing people for governments, businessmen, and whoever needed someone exterminated, and had the moolah to pay Jay for his services. He worked through an underground network accessed only through a secret source known only by a few people Jay trusted. All that cloak-and-dagger stuff. As for the wife and sister-in-law, Shidler killed them right after Roger called him, telling him that Joseph had died and he was to start on his way to Falcon City. He made it look like Islamic terrorists did it just to buy enough time for him to kill the Bowles family and get out of the country once and for all. McKenzie was shocked to learn that Dominick had become an assassin."

"So, how did Roger find him in the first place?"

"Like I said earlier, Roger knows people in high, sometimes shady, places. He knew people who could replace real medicine with placebos. And he knew people in Washington, D.C. When he found out about the deal between Joseph and Stefano, Roger began to wonder what had happened to Dominick. Roger had a connection in the Justice Department who told him, after being paid a handsome amount, about what happened to Dominick after he turned on his father. After he left the Army, the government lost track of him. The deal they had made with Dominick was that they would no longer keep tabs on him once he was out of the Army, but he had to keep the name Jay Shidler. He and they figured that all those with the DeFranco organization who might want him dead were in prison for life or dead themselves. So, this guy at Justice didn't know where Shidler was presently, so Roger did what most of us would do next."

"He went to Google."

"Yep. Took him a while, but he finally found a Jay Shidler living in Flagstaff, Arizona, who he thought might be the guy he was looking for."

"But Roger didn't know about Jay being a freelance assassin, did he?"

"No, not at first. He did a little more digging and found out about Jay's impressive war record, his abilities to kill other people, as well as underground rumors that he had gone from American soldier to assassin for hire. Once he found all that out, Roger figured Jay would be the perfect guy to do the job. Plus, the perfect symmetry of it all—the son of Stefano DeFranco killing the son of Joseph Bowles. The deal would be consummated after all. So, he flew out to Flagstaff, staked out Jay's house, and finally encountered him one evening."

"Must have been an interesting meeting."

"Indeed. Roger told Jay who he was and what he wanted. He told Jay he knew about the deal between Stefano and Joseph, which was the first time Jay had ever heard about it."

"How much did Roger offer Jay?"

"One million dollars, to be delivered into a numbered Swiss bank account."

"Damn. Bet there was no hesitation in Jay's reply."

"Nope. This was a month ago. Since then, they have been laying the groundwork for the plan. The video they released on the Internet was an actual execution. However, it was manipulated, so you couldn't tell exactly who was being killed. It was to be assumed that it was Jay Shidler being killed by Boko Haram, but in reality, it was soldiers from the Nigerian Army killing off a terrorist they had apprehended. Shidler had done a job for the Nigerian government, and this was payback for that. Roger and Jay worked out the plan for Jay to drive from Flagstaff to Falcon City when the time came to execute the kill. Avoiding leaving behind a paper trail of credit card purchases along the way, only using cash, provided by Roger."

"Then we know the rest."

"All too well, buddy."

"What about Shidler killing his wife and sister-in-law? Was that part of the plan, too?"

"According to Roger, no. Call it an audible on Shidler's part. Call it two unlucky ladies being in the wrong place at the wrong time. Shidler couldn't let them live. Same case with those two sheriff's deputies outside the house."

"And just like Andrea." Randall closed his eyes, taking it all in. "So, what's going to happen to Roger? To the newspaper?"

"Roger is going to be in prison for a very long time. Conspiracy to commit murder isn't exactly a misdemeanor. Not just Bryan and his family but his father, as well. With his dad, it's much closer to actual murder."

"Why do you think he confessed?"

"He didn't have much choice in the matter. Holbrook confessed to everything that he had heard Roger say about the matter, such as hiring Wendell Shane to break into your house. He didn't know about the bigger plot. But I think the fact that the plan failed discouraged Roger enough to confess all. I don't know how much it will help him with his sentencing, but his confession was the lesser of two shitty choices. As for the future of the newspaper, I have no idea. His wife and kids are in seclusion somewhere, understandably. As far as I know, Joseph's change to his will, giving Bryan half the paper, is legal now. Guess it's up to Bryan how he wants to handle it."

"How are he and his family?"

"Shaken, but they'll be okay. Bryan has been here at the hospital a lot over the last few days, checking in on you."

"He saved my life."

"That he did," Kayla revealed a dry grin. "Think about it, Randy—Dominick DeFranco escaped being killed by his father, then spent years in Afghanistan being incessantly shot at by the Taliban and al-Qaeda, just to spend years as a hired assassin, nearly without a scratch. So, who ends up punching his ticket? A cartoonist from western New York. Life is sometimes just plain fucking goofy, isn't it?"

Randall smiled. "Indeed."

"Before I go, there is one other thing I wanted to show you to further prove my point. The police found a letter in Jay Shidler's vehicle. It was in a duffel bag, with clothes, guns, ammo, etc." He reached into his jacket and withdrew an envelope. "I thought I would share it with you." Kayla took out the letter and unfolded it. "It's dated December 11, 2002. It reads:

"'Hello, Mr. DeFranco. We have never met, but I am sure that you have heard of me. My name is Joseph Bowler, and I am the owner and publisher of the *Falcon City Expression* newspaper. I know that you are testifying for the government in your father's case. I wanted to thank you for doing this, though I realize it must not have been an easy decision for you. However, your father was responsible for the deaths of two of my journalists in Buffalo, New York, in 1982. Their names were Eric Owens and Mark Paulsen. Your father is a despicable human being who has caused so much suffering for so many people. Me included. He has tried to destroy my life, but because of the brave stand you are taking, he can no longer do that. I'm sure that because of your testimony, you will have to start a new life with a new name and location. I know we will never meet, but I thank you from the bottom of my heart for your actions. You possess bravery and a sense of integrity that I truly admire, especially considering that your decision has destroyed the DeFranco family. May you have a long and happy life, and I hope you have the best holiday season possible. Joseph Bowles.'"

"Dear God. He never knew. He never knew that the man he wrote that letter to would try to destroy Bryan and his family after all."

"The irony must have pleased Dominick to no end. Which is probably why he carried it with him."

"Wonder if he ever showed it to Roger?"

"I brought up the letter to Roger, even showed it to him. Said it was the first he'd ever seen or heard about it."

"What was his reaction?"

"He laughed. The only smile I saw on his face during the interview."

Kayla had left, and Randall had gone back to sleep. He wasn't sure how many hours later it was, but he woke up to see Bryan standing by his bed.

"Back from the near dead. Nice to see you, Randy. Your sister said coming in and seeing you for a few minutes was okay."

"Nice to see you, too, Bryan. How are you? How is your family?"

"They're doing okay under the circumstances. The last few days have been rough, but we'll get through it. How are you doing?"

"Been better. But they say I'm going to recover."

"Good."

"Thank you for what you did. He was going to kill me. I was helpless to do anything."

"You bought us time, Randy—even though you ended up in a bad way. You kept him from killing us all."

"What was happening with you guys in the basement while I was fighting with Dominick?"

"The basement is pretty spacious. I got Emily and the kids into a bathroom at the far end. We could hear the commotion upstairs, but I wasn't sure who was fighting whom. However, I was worried. I decided to take matters into my own hands. Emily and the kids begged me not to go back up, but I assured them I'd be okay. I told them to stay quiet, and I went out and found the gun I had hidden in a cabinet. I had one in the basement and one in mine and Emily's bedroom. I loaded the gun and eased my way back up the steps without my shoes so he couldn't hear me. I disengaged the safety on the gun, unlocked and cracked open the basement door just in time to see Dominick heading toward you with the knife. That was when I opened the door all the way and shot him."

"I should have been the one to kill him. He kicked my ass, Bryan. Look at me lying here all bandaged and plastered up. I've never had that happen before. I met someone whose skills were so beyond mine that I didn't have a chance. The worst part is that I let him get into my head with him talking smack about Andrea. And it almost got you and your family killed, along with me. I should have done better by you."

"Stop that! I'm alive. My family is alive. You're alive. The man who tried to kill us is dead. And the man who hired him —my fucking brother—is going to spend the rest of his fucking life in prison."

"How do you feel about that? I mean, deep down. He is your brother, after all."

"In blood and name only. Not in my heart."

"Joe Kayla told me about your father's change to his will. What are you going to do?"

Bryan sighed. "Well, as far as the newspaper goes, I still want nothing to do with it. Never have, never will. But I will take advantage of my father's change of heart. I'm selling off the shares of the stocks I am receiving and putting all of it into a college fund for my kids. By the time they get there, I hate to think of what it will cost." Bryan paused. "That being said, I hope you're still around to teach them somewhere. I would be honored. Thank you for all you did for my family and me. You might not believe it, but you saved our lives. And, yeah, I saved yours. I think your sister is my new number one fan."

Randall laughed, but not too hard—it was too painful to do so. "I promise she won't go Annie Wilkes on you. She's the best. I'm glad she let you come in to see me."

"I've been thinking over the last few days about how I could pay you back for all you've done for my family and me. Your sister and I were talking earlier, and she mentioned you didn't have a literary agent at the moment. Is that right?"

"Yeah, that's right."

"Look, I haven't read any of your work yet, but from what I've heard, you have a great talent. What I wanted to do was get you in contact with my agent. Her name is Samantha Matthews. She's been very beneficial to me, and she knows her stuff. I'd like to get you two in touch when you are more up to it. Maybe she can get a deal for you, so you wouldn't have to self-publish anymore. That way, you could have more financial freedom to do research and write full-time or closer to it than you have been. Would you be interested in that?"

Randall was pleasantly surprised and touched by Bryan's offer. "Yeah, of course. Thank you, Bryan."

"Don't mention it. Like I said, I wanted to thank you for helping us out, and I thought that maybe getting you an agent would help you take that writing dream of yours to the next level. I'll contact her later and get back to you. Listen, I'm going to get out of here. Not allowed to stay too long. But I will come back to visit soon." Bryan took Randall's unbroken right hand. "Get better soon. And thank you again for everything. I am sorry about your friend and about the two deputies who were killed outside my home. That will be on my mind for the rest of my life. All of them died for no reason—all because of my fucking brother and Stefano DeFranco's son."

"Yeah. They will be on my mind, too. But I don't hold you responsible. You were a victim as much as they were...as was I."

"He said something after I shot him the first time. He could only whisper it, but I was close enough to him to catch it. It was in Italian. *Padre, perdonami*. When I had a moment to spare, I looked it up on Google Translate."

"My Italian is not that great. What does it mean in English?"

"It means, 'Father, forgive me.'"

"Huh. I guess the bastard had a change of heart when he realized his end had arrived. Do you forgive your father, Bryan?"

He was quiet for a moment. Then he sighed. "Not yet. But what I went through with him has made me want to be the best father I can be to my children. So, if he did leave me with a legacy, hopefully, it is that. I might not know all the right things to do, but I know what not to do. However, right now, I can't forgive him for what he did. Maybe someday, after enough time has passed, I can find it in my heart to do so. Maybe..."

An hour after Bryan had left and Randall had fallen asleep again, Rachel entered the room again. Randall wasn't that deep into sleep, and her entrance awoke him. He could see out the window that it had grown dark, an early winter darkness. That was one reason the season was not Randall's favorite.

"Sorry that I woke you. Just wanted to see you again before it got too late."

"It's okay. Been sleeping enough over the last few days."

"How are you feeling?"

"Physically or emotionally?"

"Both."

"Like shit on both counts."

"Tell me about the emotional part, babe."

Randall looked away from Rachel momentarily, staring up at the ceiling. "For the first time in my life, I doubt myself in my martial arts abilities. I've never fought anyone with the skills Jay Shidler had. Or Dominick DeFranco, I should say. I was taught by some of the best in the business, Rachel. This guy was on another level, and I almost died. I almost allowed Bryan and his family to die in the process. We all would be dead now if it weren't for Bryan's bravery."

"For which I will be forever grateful to him. You had no idea what you were getting into."

"But I fucking should have! Dominick played not only physically but mentally with me as well. I went into that fight not in the best mental frame of mind." Randall stopped, gathering his emotions. "I just had seen the body of a dear friend lying in my living room, killed in my home. Someone who shouldn't have died. She was innocent."

"I know, babe. And I'm so sorry. I know when you two were more than friends, I was rather hard on you about it. I'm sorry about that. It was never anything personal toward her. I know she was a wonderful young lady, and you cared for her deeply. I'm sorry for those two cops who Shidler killed as well. Or DeFranco. Whatever the fuck his name was. This whole affair was one big mess, and I almost lost my brother because of it."

"I know. I think once I get better, I'm going to teach and write full-time. I think I've had enough of the PI game. Losing someone like Andrea, who had so much potential to do great things in the field of history, and myself almost losing my life, has made me realize that there is too much I want to do. I have to allow myself the time to do it. When Bryan was here earlier, he brought up the notion of hooking me up with his agent. Maybe getting something worked out like that would give me more time and freedom to write."

Rachel didn't say anything at first but then said, "Well, it's your decision, of course. But I won't lie—I don't want you to be a private investigator anymore or have anything else to do with danger or violence. You went into it in the first place because you felt you had to do something to make Pam's death mean something positive. As much as you have tried to do that, I don't think that's completely possible. You gave it your best shot. She's still gone, and all those potential years we were supposed to have with her are only a lost goal, and they will stay that way. I think it's time to do what you do best. Teach. Write. Be the next David McCullough, or whoever. Be Randall Arthur. Be who that guy is supposed to be, what you were born to be. And, no, you weren't born to be a private investigator, or an undercover DEA agent, or a hero against crime in general. You were drawn into that because of a tragedy that angered you and broke your heart. You were born to teach and write about the past so others would learn from it and understand what we did right and wrong. Bryan told me he wanted to see if his agent might represent you. If that happens, I think it would be wonderful. I want you to know that Larry and I will always be there for you. Not just in the next few months, helping you get well again, but even after that. We're family. Forever."

"I appreciate that more than words, babe. I love you. Both of you. I want you guys to be together and happy if that's what you both truly want."

"It is. He's been amazing to me, not just over the last few days but always. This feels right, Randy. He wanted me to let you know that he loves you and he will see you soon. He's been here with me the whole time you've been here since Saturday. He was so exhausted, so I made him go get some rest. I told him I would get some too, which I'm about to do. The doctors say you'll be okay, so I'm going home to get some sleep."

"Good. I'll be okay. Go home and rest. I'll see you tomorrow. I love you."

Rachel lightly kissed her brother on the lips. "I love you, too. And if you ever do this to us again, I will really hurt you."

Randall smiled. "No doubt. Goodnight, Rachel."

"Goodnight. Sleep well. If you need us, let the nurses know, and they will contact us, okay?"

"I will."

Rachel left the ICU room, and Randall was alone once again. Except for the nurses, he would have no more visitors for the night. Randall knew he had a daunting rest of the winter to endure. He had already borne so much that he wished he could have escaped. But there would inevitably be more to come. Arduous physical therapy here at the hospital, full of pain, sweat, and impatient frustration with a slow speed of progress. He would also be dealing with the repercussions of the death of his young, beautiful friend, so full of potential, a bright and prosperous life snuffed out in an instant just because of horrible timing. Not to mention having to deal with the shame of being bested by another expert in martial arts so decisively, nearly dying at his hands if not for Bryan Bowles coming to the rescue at the last second.

Randall had accepted this case of the broken father and his outreach to a son he had abandoned not once but twice—first by allowing him and his family to be sentenced to a pointless and violent death and then by discarding that son from the family altogether, just because his dream did not harmonize with his father's. Randall had accepted this case with professional confidence that he could find the answers that Bryan was looking for, that he could find a solution, and that all would come out well. He had entered this case with the confident ego of an intelligent investigator. Instead, he left it damaged, both physically and emotionally, questioning whether he should even follow this line of business in the first place, even in a part-time fashion. Randall would have plenty of time to ponder his future and make a final decision, but right now, lying in a hospital bed in a condition such as he had never suffered, he seriously believed he would never want to take another case as a private investigator again. He would do what he and his beloved twin sister truly believed he was born to do—to teach and write history for those who hungered for knowledge about humanity's past. That was the true love of his heart at the moment. He would just be a professor and a writer and try to make the rest of his life as happy and meaningful as possible. He would leave the risking of life and limb to others who had the vital passion for it he no longer felt.

Yes, it would be a long rest of winter, but he also knew he had his family to be there for him as he lived through the struggles of what was to come. His twin sister and Larry Carter, whom he thought of in the recesses of his heart as his brother—he knew they would have his back and make sure that he was not alone. He knew he had the loving support of people who had him in their hearts forever. And that is what family truly is—unconditional love and support, always through the good and the bad, through the successes and the mistakes. It didn't matter if it came from those who shared the same DNA or a good friendship. As Randall had so cruelly discovered in the process of this case, the DNA family did not always mean a true family. Bryan Bowles had learned that lesson more than once. But Randall knew that Bryan and his true family would be all right.

Because of love.

Randall also knew that winter would not last that much longer. Because soon, the bleak skies, short days, cold temperatures, and irksome icy precipitation falling like mass confetti from the clouds above would transition with the progress of the Earth on its axis around the sun to steadily longer days, warmer temperatures, and the budding of trees and plants that had been bare as skeletons for the last few bleak and frigid months. It would be a rebirth of nature, and Randall hoped it would also mean a rebirth of his body and spirit.

Like the light observable at the end of a long, dark tunnel, spring was on the horizon.

THE END

About the Author

DeWayne Twitchell has published several mystery novels, short stories, and even poems, including *Descending Soul, Night's Plutonian Shore* (Honorable Mention in Writers of the Future), *Lone Voyager* (Honorable Mention in Writers of the Future), *Significant Other*, and *Down Under*.

DeWayne lives currently lives in Arkansas.

linkedin.com/in/dewayne-twitchell-203635160

Milton Keynes UK
Ingram Content Group UK Ltd.
UKHW021936281024
450365UK00018B/1122